THE GIRL WITH TWO-TONED EYES

RAJA ISHFAQ SOHIL

SCAN ME

WITH DEEP GRATITUDE

I would like to extend my deepest gratitude to everyone who has been part of this journey, in ways big or small.

First and foremost, I owe everything to my parents. To my mother, my first teacher, my companion- your love and wisdom have shaped me into the person I'm today. To my father my guiding pillar and constant source of strength- your dreams for me have inspired and motivated me every day.

I also want to sincere appreciation to my siblings. You've always been my cheerleaders, supporting me with your love, encouragement and belief in me.

I am who I am today, Alhamdullilah, thanks to the Almighty and the unwavering support of parents and teachers. It is their guidance and wisdom that have shaped me and helped me grow.

This novel, though a work of fiction, it is a product of countless moments of imagination, observations, and understanding.

I hope this story resonates with readers, offering a glimpse into the worlds we create through imagination.

Thank you for believing in me, for guiding me, and for being a constant source of inspiration.

One

The year was 1960. A cold winter in December had settled over the small village in *Kahsar Pur*, above Sonamarg, a mysterious village near the mountains, its air heavy with the chill of winter, sinking deep into every soul.

At exactly five in the evening, in the dimly lit home of Khwaja Hassan, a cry split the silence. A girl ***Noor*** was born, distinguished by a unique feature: her eyes. One was a striking cat-eye color, inherited from her mother, while the other was a more common brown. This condition, known as heterochromia, is quite rare, occurring in only 1% of the population.

In Hassan's traditional, patriarchal family, the birth of a girl felt like tempest, a calamity that had arrived without warning.

Hassan lived in modest, four-room house, each room a spacious twenty by fifteen feet, connected in U shape around a barren courtyard. There was no terrace, and in that empty space, the family often kindled a clay hearth which they called *"Chula"* for cooking during summers. One corner was piled high with firewood, saved carefully for these biting winter months. Inside

Dayi Zainab, the family midwife was assisting Hassans wife Maryam through the throes of labor.

Dayi Zainab was a highly respected woman in the village. She was known for her missing four front teeth and the faint scent of snuff locally called *"Naswar"* on her breathe whenever she smiled. It is estimated that she had delivered babies and assisted all the 123 households in our village. Once, when I asked her about the exact number she laughed and said "*chowbis, pachis*" and it just keeps going in a loop. I later realized I was probably the 31st or 32nd maybe.

She always wore a yellow shawl with an embroidered border, with a woven scarf on her head and the shawl dropped over her shoulders. When I once asked her about the shawl–She said that this shawl was the last memory she had of her mother. It was the most precious thing to her.

Dayi Zainab was a widow who lived alone, with no children nearby. Her house was a single-room structure. Inside there was a white goat and its kid separated from the rest of the room by a wooden partition. Dayi slept on a cot *"charpai"* (I heard *Khatt* for the same thing from my mother.) on the other side of the partition. Her kitchen utensils were hung on wooden pegs on stone wall, and in front of the *charpai* there was hearth whose chimney called as *"Bukhari"* extended through the mud wall. This was a small restroom type which can afford only two or three persons at a time was all she needed. What more she possibly wants? She spent her entire days visiting the village women in their homes and would return to her own home in the evenings to tend to her goats, as there was always a fear of lions, despite nobody actually saw but the villagers, however, had seven or ten encounters with leopards. She usually got Yahya and Muqeem her nephews to do this task for her but when they were off playing near the wild olive tree *"Khaw"* she had to do it herself.

Maryam, writhing in agony, let out piercing screams.

"Sabar Jigar" Dayi whispered her voice steady comfort. "Have patience my dear."

Outside Hassans entire family waited with baited breath, eyes fixed on the door, hoping for the cries of baby boy.

Maryam, meanwhile, lay drenched in pain, hot tears streaming down her cheeks like a hidden stream breaking loose from years of captivity.

I had heard about my mother's family from Dayi, who often spoke of my grandparents and relatives, though my mother rarely mentioned them.

Dayi used to say that my mother and father's marriage had been a compromise, a match arranged by circumstance more than by choice. Half of my mother's family had migrated to Azad Kashmir a region occupied by Pakistan and my maternal grandparents had passed away just a year after her marriage.

My mother, Maryam Jahan, was a tall woman with piercing, catlike eyes and cheeks the color of dawn. She had been married young, right after finishing her "Amparah" (an Arabic book for memorizing short surahs of Quraan) with Maulana Rashid, when she barely had the chance to dream beyond her books. Besides this my mother knew reading and writing Urdu as well.

I had always glimpsed buried dreams in her eyes– unspoken desires that never found words, bound forever within her gaze.

On that day December evening, as snow blanketed Gulmarg in a vast, white sheet and the biting wind lashed every corner of the valley, Maryam's cries filled the air. In another room, Hassan, dressed in traditional *phiran,* warmed himself beside an *angeethi*, softly humming a Kashmiri raag, his breaths punctuated by deep drags on his *Jhajri* (Hookah). Plumes of smoke curled from his thick lips, escaping through the thick mustache and beard that framed his stern face. The gurgling sound of the hookah: *gud gud gud...* reached Maryam's ears, drawing her mind away with every beat of *gud gud,* back into her own distant memories, even as the intense pain began pulling her toward a state close to unconsciousness. But every now and then, Dayi Zainab would land a sharp slap on her cheek to keep her awake.

"Maryam! Just a little more strength!" Dayi shouted, clutching Maryam's hand with one hand while applying pressure to her belly with the other.

"Bismillah!"

Maryam's voice erupted in one final, heart-wrenching scream. Her fingers clawed at the blanket beneath her, as if tearing into it could drain all the pain from her body. Then, a loud cry split the air, not hers, but the cry of a newborn child. Everyone rushed towards Dayi's temporary labor room, anticipation igniting their steps. A single oil "Diya" (Lamp) flickered near the *roshandan,* ventilator, its light casting soft shadows and filling the room with a thick comforting scent, which I was addicted to.

Hassan's voice rumbled from behind the crowd:

"Abdullah..." he began the name trailing off with expectations.

But before anyone could approach, Dayi's voice rang out, commanding respect, "Get out, all of you! Don't you have the decency to honor the purdah?"

Inside the room, Maryam lay semi-conscious her mind swaying between reality and a dream. She feared one thing alone: What if it's a girl?

Meanwhile Dayi bent close, her warm breath tickling the Maryam's ear as she whispered,

"Mubarak... another Maryam has arrived."

Those words drifted into Maryam's ears, each syllable laced with warmth, yet each burning like hot coals. Her entire body went limp, and tears began streaming down her face once more, silent yet fierce, like a river too long dammed.

Moments later the family members were allowed inside. Hassan was the first to step forward. His face, hard with years of life, bore a thick mustache, heavy brows, and a beard that made him appear at least two dozen years older than Maryam, although he was sixteen years her elder. He looked down his newborn daughter with a gaze as cold as winter air, his expression turning as if he was inspecting something distasteful.

And in that fleeting moment, Maryam felt her heart break a thousand times over. Her child, who was not a son, had entered a world that may never welcome her warmth.

Two

The last days of October 1962 were cold and dry, with yellow leaves scattered over the brown fields, and a light frost dusted the nearby hills.

Our village was a blend of cultures, with refugees from Baluchistan, Azad Kashmir and native Kashmiris living together. Among the villagers, there was only one person whom everyone respectfully called "Subedar". A retired soldier, he owned a small shop built from stones and wood.

Subedar was known for his heavy *"charas"* hashish use; his eyes was always half-closed and bloodshot, while his thick, twisted mustache curved like the horns of an ox. His shop had stone walls, plastered with mud, in which a tiny piece of mirror, no larger than a matchbox, was embedded. Subedar would often glance at it to twist and groom his mustache. He always had a beedi (a local hand-rolled cigarette) smoldering between his fingers. Outside his shop, a large dried trunk of deodar tree about ten to twelve feet long, lay peeled and polished. Serving as a bench for villagers.

The shop was gathering spot for people, where they'd come to buy tobacco for their *"Jhajris"*, talk and listen to the gossip of the day. Nearby, a small spring trickled past, its path running close to the shop. In front of the shop a wooden pole with a thin silver wire wrapped around it, supporting a dusty weathered radio hanging from it. The radio its dials coated with a decade's worth of grime, produced cracking sounds, sometimes loud and sometimes barely audible, as if the news was echoing from a far-off place. People often came to Subedar's to catch the latest broadcast from *Akashvani* and to purchase small rations or, as my mother once mentioned, to "watch the women".

One of the regulars was Afzal, my father's younger brother, who was six years younger than him, known to everyone as "Dhulki." He was round, with no distinguishable neck, just a fleshy mass from face to shoulders, much like a drum.

Whenever he looked at the woman, his gaze would settle first on chest, then her face. I learned this from my mother one day when we were fetching water.

According to Dayi Ammi, Afzal was an exceptionally intelligent child, even more so than Hassan, and after him, there had been a little sister who tragically passed away at the tender age of three. She died in a heart-wrenching accident when she fell from a white mare– a mare Afzal often rode with childlike pride.

One fateful day, Afzal's mother Haleema and Hassan went to the village watermill, entrusting Afzal to care for his younger sister. Afzal, full of youthful excitement, decided to share his joy of riding with her. He placed her on white mare, and they trotted around the *aangan.* But then, in an instant, joy turned to calamity. The mare, startled and unbridled, bolted toward the rugged village paths. Afzal and his sister were thrown off. The little girl hit her head on a sharp rock, her life extinguished in the blink of an eye.

This tragedy left an indelible scar on Afzal's soul. His one-vibrant demeanor faded as he retreated to himself, haunted by guilt and loss. The grief deepened when his mother, unable to bear the pain of losing her daughter, also passed away. Misfortunes followed closely– livestock perished, fields fell barren, and whispers spread through the village: Afzal is *manhoos,* cursed, the cause of every misfortune.

As the years passed, Afzal grew heavier, his body reflecting the burden of rejection and isolation. He dreamed of marrying Shabana Aapi, hoping love might redeem him, but his proposal was dismissed for a trivial scar on his lip– a flaw the village magnified beyond reason. Family after family refused him, branding him unworthy, cursed and broken. With every rejection, Afzal's spirit darkened. Once a bright and intelligent boy, he became a shadow of himself, consumed by guilt, alienation, and growing belief in his own villainy. The boy who once hoped to belong now wore the mask of a man the village had cast aside.

"Once, when I was returning from the spring with a water pot", Ammi recalled,

"Afzal stared at me and murmured, 'Still swaying, aren't you? Looks like Hassan still has some work to do. I ignored him, but he kept watching, his eyes following me until I disappeared around the bend in the path. Afzal would then give obscene gesture, bending forward, positioning his arm between his legs, and moving up and down like a bouncing ball, before heading back to Subedar's shop".

The shop had basic goods– a few sacks of rice, tea and some bottles of toffees in various colors. There were also cardboard boxes filled with stuff and tin cans filled with oil and dalda. A green plastic bottle with a yellow lid held a particular type of dried mushrooms coated with white layer probably soaked in honey called *"dhingri"*. The villagers mostly grew their own grains– lentils, maize and wheat– which they'd grind at a local mill called *"Gharat"* not far from the village owned by Gafar Chacha, a man with black beard sprinkled with white hairs here and there and always wore a turban on his head. He mostly stayed at his mill, and we would usually only see him on special occasions, especially during Eid. Men would bring their sheep and goat-skin bags filled with grains, slung over their shoulders, to this mill.

During the 1962 war, the village men would spend entire days at Subedar's shop. Some would leave for work with their mules, others with goats or cattle, but in those two months, a spirit of freedom and relief filled the air. My mother would often say, "those two months felt like a burden lifted from our chests."

Every evening, a mullah named Bashir-ul-Haq would come to the village's Eidgah to teach the children. I, too, learned my first prayers and "Noorani Qaida" from him. The days were going shorter, and the sun no longer set between the two hills in the west but now sank behind the thick forest, casting an early darkness over the valley.

One day, Hayat kaka my paternal aunt's son overheard mullah Bashir saying, "the Chinese have taken our land". The news spread like wildfire through the village, reaching the women in their secluded homes, restricted by boundaries of tradition. They were expected to bear children, care for household, and stay within four walls. Only the men, with their white beards, attended prayers, as if age had given them right.

There was a wooden bridge nothing more than two deodar logs, worn and uneven, placed together with wooden few strips. It hung over the stream like a forgotten memory, creaking under the weight of those who crossed. The water below, sharp and bitter from the winter's chill, flowed relentlessly, carrying with it all that had been lost — or perhaps, all that had been left behind.

On a cold morning, Farooq, carrying a sack of wheat to Gafar Chacha's *gharat,* slipped from the bridge. His cry was swallowed by the rushing water, and by the time the villagers pulled him out, his leg was shattered. He lived, but there was no escaping the weight that would follow him. Rumors spread that it was her mother's fault; in her obsession with Ashraf– the monkey man with the henna-red beard and hair dyed fiery red. Ammi used to say, "some people get caught in the webs they don't even see, and some of those webs, they hold a bit of truth — and sometimes, just a whole lot of nothing."

In Kahsar Pur, it was always the woman who bore the blame. The child's fall, the man's mistake — always, the mother, the wife. It was a heavy thing, this unspoken rule, this game of blaming the weakest. But beneath the harsh words, there was a silent truth that no one dared say aloud: the village was a living thing, and its women were not its only scapegoats.

Among the many unsolved mysteries, one was the secret of the *Raaz Gufa*– up past the last of the village huts, hidden by *Sulai*– Buckthorn jungle, stood a great boulder. Beneath it lay a cave, and it was said that no married woman should pass by it, for it was cursed. Ammi once told me, in that voice she saved for the darkest truths, "There are things buried there, things deeper than the earth. No woman who dares to pass will ever walk the same again."

The mystery of that cave hung in the air like an unsolved puzzle, one no one dared to touch. No one spoke of it openly, but the weight of its silence was always there, like a shadow cast over the village. What truths lay buried there? No one knew. No one sought to find out, for the fear of what might be revealed was greater than the mystery itself.

West of village, surrounded by a wooden fence lay the *Kabristan* (graveyard). It was a quiet, somber field, visited only when there was a burial. Dayi Ammi, would often recall the sad memory of my mother's pregnancy that year. She was expecting, but the child did not survive. They buried the little body with a small grave, just beside the graveyard's edge, where my mother had placed it herself.

Three

This was the time when I was probably the age of left-hand fingers and the thumb and *Shahadat finger*, the index finger of right hand– during prayer, in the last rak'ah, it is raised once while reciting, *"Ashhadu an La illaha illallah wa Ashhadu anna Muhammadan Abduhu wa Rasuluh".*

In our village, two tall figures arrived– a man and a woman– unlike anyone else from our village. They wore long, hunter-style shoes, similar to the ones that Subedar Dada usually wore for weddings and Eid. However, these were slightly different. Hunter shoes, with large buckled bags on their backs, walking sticks in hand, and black *ainak* over their eyes. All the village kids followed behind them, while I sat in our *aangan* on the corner stone, carving the *"Kanzalwan"* pine fatwood with an axe, where the path curved towards Rahim Dada's place. Rahim Dada was the village's bone mechanic. If you broke something, he'd fix it, but with a twist– like Yahya, whose arm hasn't folded at the elbow since Rahim Dada worked his magic!

I had never seen Baba with Ammi like this man walked with his wife, arm over her shoulder, just like Yahya and Muqeem would. Maybe Baba and Ammi weren't friends; that's why Baba married a second time.

Many people gathered in our *aangan*, Ammi in the *Siyah Bhakt* room. Yes, this was the same room where Dayi would say I was born.

In this room, apart from me and Ammi, only Dayi would sometimes come, and no one else ever entered. Somedays white *suhaga,* residue left after wood burns, would be placed at our room's door.

Ammi used to say, "These are Parveen's task," as Parveen hated me and would beat me for no reason when Ammi was not around. She would warn, "Stay away from it. You will not touch it or clean it. It will harm you; it will dissolve the flesh of your body."

Parveen was Baba's second wife, her nose was long and sharp, her eyes small. She was Baba's friend; Baba always worked with her and stayed with her.

Sometimes, when Parveen would go to her father Gani's house, Baba would grab Ammi by the arm in a very disgraceful way and take her to his room. Ammi would always return from his room in tears, her face marked with scars– sometimes bite marks, sometimes slap marks. Baba would curse Ammi, and for some reason, he did the same to me.

Ammi would say, "Noor, you are the light of my eyes, that's why only I have Noor, not others," and I would always reply,

"Do you see through my right eye, the one like yours?" I had seen it in the mirror on the wall of Subedar Dada's shop– just like Ammi's eye.

She would respond "Yes *Jigar,* I see everything through that eye."

One morning, I woke Ammi to go for a pee when *Baang* my rooster, crowed. Our *Gusal Khana,* bathroom was on the left side of the house near the naalah, with walls on two sides, made of wood, open to the sky above, and a door made of pine branches which I couldn't open on my own.

When Ammi opened the *Siyah Bakht* door, there was a faint light outside, and my foot stepped into the *suhaga.* For the first time, I saw Ammi's startled face– big cat eyes, hair flowing over her face. She was more beautiful than the woman I had seen on the *mehandi,* henna packet at Subedar

Dada's shop, the one with open hair. Her lips were slightly reddish because Ammi always cleaned her teeth with walnut *miswak*. Her eyes, eyebrows, nose, chin and reddish cheeks– everything about her was beautiful. Her teeth completely white, not like mine or Dayi's.

She immediately picked me up, took me towards *Gusal Khana,* washed my foot first with water, then with mud and again with water. We both started to pee, and I sat with my legs spread, the sound of my pee came out like a whistle, just like Muqeem whistles by putting two fingers in his mouth to call the goats.

Ammi slapped my head and scolded, "Noor! Pee with your legs together. If you sit with your legs open like that while peeing *Shaitaan* will make whistle like noise and call *Rantas,* female ghost and then *Rantas* will take you far away from me. You know, your Ammi is alive for you– would you want your Ammi to die?

I replied softly, "You mean to say that you'll sleep in the graveyard with angels?"

"Yes, Ammi is alive because of Noor."

Shaitaan! I wasn't sure if she was talking about Afzal. Because whenever I've heard Ammi say Afzal's name, she always adds *"shaitaan"* at the end– Afzal shaitaan. But this time, she just said *"shaitaan."*

Looking toward Ammi, I asked, "Afzal?"

"Shhhh……. Hurry up and pee. This place is heaven for *shaitaan*."

After that, Ammi took out an old, worn-out sky colored container– it looked like it was centuries old– and filled it with water from the *bowli* in front. This *bowli* had been made by digging a small pit in the ground, and water would flow into it from the rain. Sometimes Ammi would also fill it with water from *matka*.

She made *wuzu,* ablution, and showed me how to clean myself: use your left hand and wipe, and pour water with your right. She warned, if you're not cleaned properly, *shaitaan* will take you far away from me.

Ammi was crying in the *Siyah Bhakt* room, and I lay my head in her lap, watching the tears streaming from her eyes, like the rain dripping from our *bukhari* during monsoon.

Whenever I watched the droplets falling from the above, it felt like the ground is moving upward toward the sky. But Ammi's tears didn't feel that way. Maybe she was crying because her

Sultan sheep, pure white as snow with a black spot on his forehead– like the black soot from the *Chula,* Ammi would apply near my left eyebrow– had been sacrificed.

Sometimes, I would get up climb onto the small deodar log, which Ammi would sometimes place behind the door. From there I would peek through *roshandan* watching people in the *aangan,* the noise of visitors coming to eat and leaving.

After a while, I heard knock at the door. I hurried towards it and saw a thick stick wedged behind the door. Ammi said it was to keep Afzal, Baba's cousin, from coming to harm us.

I looked towards Ammi, who quickly lifted her kameez, wiped her tears with it. And warned me in soft voice before opening the door, "Noor Jigar don't tell anyone you saw anything."

Ammi opened the door, and I knew it had to be Dayi Amma, as no one else ever came into this room. Dayi came in carrying a *thali,* platter of rice and *maaz,* meat. The aroma of *maaz* filled my nose– it was kind of meal we only had on Eid and marriages.

Dayi placed the *thali* on the floor; Ammi and Dayi sat in the corner by the *roshandan* talking, while I sat near the platter, waiting for Ammi to say, "Noor, start eating."

Whenever Ammi looked towards Dayi and talked, I'd quickly dip my *shahadat finger* into the gravy and suck it clean. The conversation between Dayi and Ammi seemed as long as from one Eid to next.

Then Dayi finally said, "Noor Jigar, eat from the side," and at that, I immediately grabbed a piece and started eating. In their long talk, three words echoed repeatedly, standing out from all the rest: "Maryam", "Noor" and "Sabar".

"Sabar": patience, Mulla Bashir-ul-Haq also say this word, usually followed by another: *"Sabar, Shukar".* Yes, this word became precious and special for me.

Dayi left, and Ammi hadn't taken a single bite, nor did she stop me– maybe because it was her *Sultan* and that's why she was crying.

After sometime the noise outside grew louder. I looked through the *roshandan* again and saw Baba passing by in a new black salwar kameez, with a white *saafa*, turban tied on his head, followed by people from the village: Gafar Chacha, Afzal, Rahim Dada, and many others. Baba entered other room. Behind them, a group of village women were holding a woman in a black *burqa,* hijab wearing white shoes just like Ammi's, and led her towards a separate room.

Ammi lifted me down from the window, held me close, and said, "we'll escape to the other side of the two mountains to the west, where the sun sets in summer. My Noor will play there with the fairies."

She held me close to her soft chest, kissed my forehead, and said, "My fairy will now go to the land of fairies."

She laid me in her lap, her hand moving inside my kurta, gently caressing my belly, humming the same words she used to sing to put me sleep.

"Walo myaeni poshey madano, chaar kar myon malinyo..."

"My heart yearns for you, my love, my soul's delight, my four limbs feel weary, my body frail and slight."

Four

The early whispers of winter had begun, with the mountain and land cloaked in dry, brown hue. The trees stood bare, as if the mountains had gone bald, reminiscent of how villagers used to shave the wool off sheep. In some patches, people had cut the grass so meticulously that the ground seemed to be waiting, with bated breath, for a white blanket of snow to cover it.

The time of year when villagers would gather and go to the jungles to fetch grass and wood. I didn't know that a year had *bara,* twelve months. In my mind, I divided the year into three parts: Eid, Assu– the time when villagers would cut the grass, and snow, until Ammi made me memorize it all.

One morning, early on a *Sumwar,* Monday, I was sleeping in the *Siyah Bakht*. Suddenly, I heard Parveen shouting abuses, the word *"kanjri"* pierced through my ears. Ammi was outside the room. I stepped out to see Parveen raging at Ammi.

She had a thick piece of wood, *Daang,* in her hand– the kind we generally used to tie bundles of maize grass and dry grass collected from the forest. Ammi's clay pot– used to fetch water from the spring– lay shattered near the door. This pot was gift from Dayi, bought from Karkhaan, the village where she lived before marriage.

Parveen was hurling abuses, and Baba did nothing to stop her. Instead, he picked up some utensils placed near the *Chula* and threw them at our door. Then he walked outside his room and stood there. Meanwhile, Afzal arrived and stood beside Baba.

Ammi held my hand tightly and firmly said, "Noor, go inside." Just as Ammi spoke, Parveen charged towards her and struck her on the head with the wood. Blood started pouring down Ammi's face, and a single cry escaped her lips, *"Mojai"*. She quickly wrapped me in her arms and rushed us inside the room.

A little while later Dayi arrived. We took our utensils and went to her house.

Perhaps Parveen was unhappy about sharing meals with us. From that day, we prepared food at Dayi's house but returned to *Siyah Bakht* to sleep.

One night, after dinner, as we were walking back to our room, the full moon shone brightly in the sky. Ammi asked me to sit on the stone. She always had a way of making the simplest things seem magical. That night, under the soft glow of the moon, her words wrapped around me like a warm quilt. "Noor," she said, her voice steady and calm, "we have to be like this moon—silent and radiant."

I stared up at the moon, its light spilling across the courtyard like a silver river. Silent and radiant? I didn't understand. "Why, Ammi? What does the moon have to do with me?" I asked, tilting my head, the curiosity in my voice betraying my impatience.

"Because, Jigar, the moon teaches us *sabar*—patience," she replied, her gaze fixed on the sky as if she could see beyond it. "God rewards patience and burns every shaitaan in hell. But patience doesn't just mean waiting. It means enduring, Noor. It means holding onto your light even when the world tries to drown you in darkness."

I frowned, still looking at the moon. It seemed so far away, so lonely. "But, Ammi," I said, my voice small, "what if the moon gets tired? What if it doesn't want to shine anymore?"

She looked at me then, her cat-like eyes— softening with a kind of love that made my chest ache. "The moon never tires, Noor. Even when the clouds hide it or the night seems too long, it's always there, waiting for its time. That's what you must learn—to be steady, even when the world seems too heavy. Your light doesn't belong to you alone; it belongs to everyone who looks up to you."

I tried to understand, but my mind kept wandering. "Does the moon like everyone, Ammi? Even shaitaan?" I asked, scrunching my nose at the thought.

Her laughter was soft, like the breeze rustling through the oak tree. "The moon doesn't choose, Noor. It gives its light to everyone—shaitaan, humans, animals, even the ones who throw stones at it. Its purpose is to shine, not to judge. And so must we. Be kind, Noor, even when it's hard. That's how you stay radiant."

Her words hung in the air, heavy and soft, like the scent of *Kachnar* in the evening. I traced circles on the ground with my toe, trying to make sense of it all. "Ammi," I said after a while, my voice barely a whisper, "what if someone breaks the moon?"

Her hand found mine, warm and steady. "No one can break the moon, Jigar. Even when it's scarred, those scars only make it more beautiful. They show that it has faced storms and survived. And so will you. Your strength is in your patience, your light in your faith. Never forget that."

I looked at her then, at the way the moonlight softened her features, and for a moment, I might have believed it, or I might not, she didn't stop until she was sure that I had started to believe that I could be like the moon—silent, radiant, and unbroken.

"Ammi," I asked, glancing up at the moon once more, "do you think it knows I'm trying to be like it?"

Her smile was small but full of pride. She pulled me close, her voice a whisper in my hair. "It knows, Noor. It always knows."

I didn't fully understand her words; I was only noticing Ammi's glowing eyes in the darkness, the reflection of the moon in those eyes, her white teeth, and the crooked smile she wore as she spoke– the moon in the sky above and the moon in Ammi's eyes below, I nodded in an agreement anyway.

Ammi and I often leave the village and take our two sheep and one goat with two kids to graze on the land nearby from where our village was no longer visible. Ammi would comb my hair, looking for lice, while teaching me *ginti,* counting on slate. I saw a figure approaching us seemed like a *deodar,* cedar log. As it came closer, I realized it was Afzal. Lying in Ammi's lap, I said, "Look, Afzal is coming." Ammi quickly sat me up, covered my head with scarf, and adjusted her posture.

When Afzal came near, his hands were behind his back. Reaching us he brought them forward, revealing *gachak,* a sweet made of mixing jaggery with groundnut, in his hands. He said, "This is for you, take it."

Without asking Ammi, I grabbed the *gachak*. Ammi didn't say a word, and I began eating siting in her lap.

Afzal then offered another piece of *gachak* to Ammi, but she refused. He lifted his eyebrows in a manner that made him look like a frog– what I had seen at the pond, and said,

"Take it. Now Hassan won't even look at you. Just say yes once, and I will take care of everything for you."

Ammi stood up, picked me up, and began walking toward a wild olive tree, *Khaw,* nearby. She held me tightly, my face over her shoulder, I saw Afzal following us. He grabbed Ammi's kameez and turn her towards him, holding her arm.

He said, "don't act so high and mighty, *Raand."* This word was new to me. He threw the *gachak* at Ammi's feet and added,

"I'll deal with you, where will you go? One day you'll come to me." With that, he walked back the same way he had come.

Ammi seated me under the olive tree, and warned me: "Noor, there are two types of people you'll encounter. Some are like Aapi, Dayi, and Dada– good people. And then there are others, like Afzal, your Baba and Parveen– shaitaans. You must protect yourself from such people. God made everyone same, but people choose to become good or bad. Always say 'yes' to what feels right and 'no' to what feels wrong." Again, she repeated it, "The wrong what Afzal shaitaan did."

Ammi taught me as much as I never learned from Mulla Bashir-ul-Haq. She asked me to recite with her, *"Allahummaghfir li wa liwaalidyyan warhamummah kama rabbayani Saghira"* – O Allah, forgive me and my parents, and have mercy on them as they raised me when I was small. She made me repeat it until it was committed to memory.

Later we return to village. Ammi left me at Dayi's house while she went to tie our goats and sheep at their place. That night, while we were cooking, I heard footsteps outside. I peeked out and saw Baba. He dropped sack at the door and left. I rushed to it, hoping it might have *gachak* or *dhingri* like

Muzamil Pupha, husband of Baba's sister, used to bring for Muqeem. But there was nothing like that.

Ammi called me and asked me to untie the knot at the corner of her scarf. Inside, she had hidden *dhingri* for me.

Our lives had split between two houses now– one for cooking, one for sleeping. Afraid of shaitaan, Ammi began placing heavy *deodar* logs against the door at night to keep it secure.

One morning, we heard Parveen crying loudly. Soon after, both Parveen and Baba left the house. Dayi told Ammi that Parveen's brother's wife had passed away– though I understood this meant she had gone to rest forever in the graveyard. Baba and Parveen had gone to bid her *alwida*– a final goodbye.

Around noon, I saw Baba returning alone. He walked straight towards us. Ammi and I were sitting in the *aangan*. For the first time, Baba grabbed my hand and looked at me. Although it was a gaze full of hatred, I felt, even if for a fleeting moment, that he might pick me up in his arms. That perhaps, like Muqeem's baba or Yahya's, he would hold me in his lap and play with me. But it was nothing more than a dream seen with open eyes. Then he turned to Ammi, grabbed her arm, and tried to pull her up. She resisted. He then barked at me, "go and get some water!" in a low voice after inhaling long breath he said, "*kanjar aulad,* daughter of a courtesan." I went inside to get water.

When I returned, I saw Baba dragging Ammi roughly towards his room. She resisted, but he was forceful. I placed the glass down and followed quietly. Baba shut the door behind him. I crouched near the door, peeking through a small crack. What I saw shook me.

Baba threw Ammi on to the floor. She was lying on her back; he slapped her repeatedly. She raised her hands to shield her face, crying. He grabbed her hair with one hand, and with the other tore her kameez, pulling it apart at the chest. He shouted, *"kanjri"* – the same word Parveen had used. "I'm your *khawand,* husband. I haven't given you Talaq. Where do you go these days? Tell me *kanjri!"* this word was unfamiliar to me but filled with venom.

Ammi cried out, "Noor! Noor! Noor!" hearing her scream, I started pounding on the door with my tiny hands, terrified. Baba heard the noise and stepped back. Ammi quietly got up, covered her chest with her hand, and came to the door. She opened it, grabbed my hand, and rushed us to Siyah Bakht.

Once inside, she bolted the door. I was trembling with fear. Ammi hugged me tightly, saying, "Noor, my life. Don't be scared Ammi is fine." For the first time, I couldn't agree with her. As she changed her torn kameez and carried me to Dayi's house, I began to realize why Ammi called them *"shaitaan."*

Five

1971- The village abuzz with rumors that Pakistani *Muhajids,* militants had started a war with Hindustan. The tension was palpable, especially since the conflict seemed close. Every morning, the men gathered near Subedar's Dada's shop to listen to the news on the radio, seeking updates with bated breath.

Ammi and I were heading toward the jungle. It was a bitterly cold day, and the frost stung our faces as we walked. After a while, I felt something wet in my pajama. A few more steps, I touched my pajama and froze when I saw blood on my hand. Terrified, I screamed, "Ammi! Blood.

Ammi was walking ahead of me, turned back abruptly. I showed her my hand– and stammered, "blood from the pajama." Her face turned pale, almost mirroring the red of the blood. She knelt down immediately and inspected me.

Her voice softened as she tried to calm me, "Noor Jigar, nothing happened." She took off her black scarf, wrapped it tightly around my pajama from the outside, and kissed my forehead. She then carefully placed her axe in the bush, ensuring it was hidden and safe and carried me on her back, rushing home. Bathed me gently, dressed me in the fresh clothes. She laid me down on Dayi's *charpai,* whispering reassurances that everything was fine. But I could see the worry lingering in her eyes, a quiet storm she tried to keep hidden. The world outside spoke of *Jung,* wars, but in that moment, my little world revolved around Ammi's comforting presence.

Ammi had now taught me all the things that she used to talk about with Dayi or Sakina Aapi, things she would always ask me to move away from. It was then that I began to realize that I had grown up.

Every day the same routine activities continued– going with Ammi to fetch water, taking our goats and sheep to graze in the nearby fields. Tahir– Sakina Aapi's son started coming along with us too. One day when Aapi was unwell, she sent Tahir to take care of the cattle. Tahir usually stayed at Gafar Chacha's *Gharat*, and sometimes Aapi would send him to the bazaar with other villagers to sell walnuts, maize, *kunzalwan*, dried mushrooms, *asraal*– wild kohlrabi, and ferns. Whenever Aapi and Ammi went to the jungle, they would spend hours talking and collecting these things, and then bring them back home to dry them.

One day, Ammi and I were eating small, dark fruits from a large thorny bush– *shamal,* I carefully picked them with two fingers, folding my Kurti's front part holding with my teeth, gathering them in it. Just then Tahir arrived, he helped me collect these fruits and sat with us.

Tahir, a shy guy, always in a salwar kameez and a red hunter shoe. His hair was parted to the right, with a curl that would often fall over his eye, and he would occasionally shake his neck to brush it away. Below his nose, he had a light mustache and he was always smiling. He was no less than a monkey, always climbing trees, making us laugh whenever we were out there.

There was just one thing– he could never pronounce any word properly, especially, starting with "Rey, R". Maybe his tongue was a bit small. Every time I would tease him, calling him, "Rahim Dada" he would say "Lahim Dada" and we would burst into laughter. He never minded it.

Perhaps *jung* was escalating. One day, Ammi and I were returning from spring water when I counted *Satra,* seventeen men heading towards our village. They were dressed in identical clothes and caps, each carrying a large iron gun slung over one shoulder. I recognized the same type of gun from a time when Afzal had accompanied five or six men to our village at night. Some of those men had long beards, others didn't but they hadn't worn matching outfits. Those men had visited every house in the village. Muqeem, Yahya and Tahir, had told me the next day that the same men had come to their houses too. They even took a small goat from Dayi. Afzal had guided them to each house.

Ammi had warned me back then, "don't talk to these people. They take away innocent people and torment them."

Among the approaching men with matching uniforms, the tallest one at the front was holding a dog. They were coming towards us, but we were still a little far from them. Ammi said, "Noor, rest here for a while. Let them pass." Before I could ask anything, Ammi added, "these are *Fojis,* soldiers from Hindustan. They protect the land from *Jung,* and attacks."

I was confused. Why would anyone fight over land? Couldn't they just live peacefully in the village? The soldiers were still some distance away when Afzal appeared from the village and came towards us, and with hatred in his voice, said to Ammi,

"Are you waiting for them? Do you think they will make you happy? He then shouted in his cracking sound, "*Dafa Kanjri–* get lost, you whore, and go home!" he stormed downhill, leaving us behind.

I watched as the fojis stopped him and questioned him. Afterward, they gave him bags to carry and some supplies. Then, they began walking towards us. Ammi instructed me, "when the fojis come close, greet them."

They reached us, sat down at the bend in the path where villagers often rested. I greeted them with raised hand said, "Salam". They all smiled warmly and greeted me back, shaking my hand one by one. Afzal stood nearby, Garling.

A man with a thick mustache shouted at Afzal, "sit down!" Afzal obeyed begrudgingly.

The soldiers asked Ammi for water. She removed the lid from her earthen pot and gestured for them to drink. Each one drank and seemed to look at me with curiosity, perhaps with my differently colored eyes. One of them lifted me into his lap and offered me a small, slightly bitter, dark treat sealed in a packet with a picture of girl and some groundnuts on it. I looked at Ammi for permission, she nodded.

Afterwards, the soldiers started questioning Ammi about the village. She pointed on its direction as she spoke.

Suddenly, Afzal shouted again, *kanjri* – you whore! Go to Hassan.

At this one of the fojis, a man with a short beard stepped forward and kicked Afzal in the back, making him fall. He grabbed Afzal's hair and snarled, "get on your knees, *kutte,* you filthy dog!" Afzal compiled, trembling under his grip.

The soldiers then told us we could leave. One of them placed the water pot back on Ammi's head, and we headed home.

The next morning, as, Ammi, Tahir and I set out for our usual routine– taking care of our goat, sheep and other chores, mingled with Tahir's playful plans, some routine complaints, and small joys– we noticed a large number of soldiers heading toward our village.

By then, I had grown old enough to start understanding the difference between the good and bad, joy and sorrow. I never played comfortably with any village kid as I did with Tahir. His silly talks and monkey-like antics would always make me laugh.

Whenever we went to the fields, Ammi would get busy with some tasks, and Tahir and I would play by building small houses out of pebbles. We would make tiny walls and place wooden sticks as *Gudda, Guddi,* dolls inside those fragile homes. Those houses were weaker than real ones, maybe because their *bunyaad,* foundation was weak.

I remember once asking Ammi why Baba didn't live with us and why he seemed to hate us while staying happy with Parveen. Ammi had replied, "Noor, you won't understand this. Some relationships have weak *bunyaad,* can never hold a strong home, no matter how grand it looks. But when the *bunyaad* is strong, even the fiercest storms, rains and snow can't shake home."

It made me realize why Shabana Baji's house had fallen. Shabana Baji was a widow. Ammi had said she was a tall with thick long hair that made her unique. Whenever she tied her hair into a braid, it would hang down below her back, adding to her distinct appearance. She was our neighbor, her house was slightly isolated, a bit away from the main *basti,* settlement, but not too far– just a few steps. Her husband Majid was handicapped and had one leg missing. Ammi told me that *muhajids,* militants wanted to marry Shabana Baji, but when Majid refused, they took him to far-off hill, threw him off, and killed him.

The militants often came to Shabana Baji's house, bringing goats, chickens and sheep from the village, cooking and eating there.

Sakina Aapi once told me that Afzal used to help them torment Shabana Baji. She always kept her head covered; I never saw her hair. Rumors said they had cut her hair off.

Perhaps the weak *bunyaad* Ammi spoke of was something like that between her and Baba. That's why Baba was happier with Parveen and Iqbal– or maybe it was because of me. Or because of Iqbal– Parveen's son, with golden hair like our goat Lali, and a perpetually runny nose. He was kind hearted, especially when playing with mud. I used to secretly watch him play.

One day, he played with me outside Siyah Bakht room. Parveen saw us. She came and hit me on my nose. That was probably the first time I saw stars in day time, and their words came true, the ones I often heard from people in the village. Darkness clouded my vision, and sparks of stars began to appear before my eyes. I fell backward, my nose bleeding profusely. From that day onward I stopped playing with Iqbal because Ammi warned me that Parveen would hurt me again. I often saw Baba bringing the best sweets for Iqbal, but he never treated me the same. Maybe Ammi was right– Baba and Ammi's *bunyaad,* was weak.

While playing, I tried teaching Tahir how to pronounce my name correctly. He often called me "Nool" instead of Noor. I taught him to take a deep breath, round his lips, and say "Noor" from his heart and belly touching his tongue upwards. But still, "Nool" would come out of his mouth. The day was entirely dedicated to

Tahir because Subedar Dada's shop was closed as he was busy assisting the fojis.

The soldiers stayed in our village for around two months and nine days. They made homes for themselves out of large cloth tied with ropes– without wood or stones. Every day, they wandered around the forest and the areas surrounding our village. During their stay, all the men in the village had to report to the soldiers both in morning and evening for *haazri,* attendance, just like Mulla Bashir-ul-Haq would take in the Eidgah.

The soldiers didn't take our goats or sheep. They only took vegetables from Sakina Aapi and chickens from villagers. Sometimes, they would show their guns. They were kind to the children but harsh on adults, often making them lie on ground and beating them with sticks on their hips, and we, the children were asked to count– *Aik do teen...* One day I counted up to *churasi, pachasi*– eighty-four, eighty-five. Ammi explained that it was because of mujahids.

I once asked her, "why do they beat us? We didn't take their land. This land belongs to our villagers. Why do they hit us?" Ammi simply replied, "Noor, don't ask too many questions, they beat us because they might have thought we are helping the mujahids–

on the other hand mujahids beat us because they think we are informing fojis."

Ammi's words were not less than a riddle for me. I was always confused. What the matter actually was, remained a mystery for me. There was something good like beating Afzal, but there was also something evil, like beating Gafar Chacha and others.

Gradually, I began understanding Ammi's description of Shaitaan.

A shaitaan is someone who takes away someone's freedom. A shaitaan is someone who oppresses and beats without a valid reason, tortures without reason like Baba like Afzal. Shaitaan is someone who doesn't let others play, like Parveen.

Now the image of shaitaan was clear to me: A shaitaan could wear a cap, have eyes and voice like Baba's, a style of beating like Parveen's, clothes like the angry foji, and hairs and deeds like the night soldiers, militants. A shaitaan could appear any time, day or night, in the cold or heat.

Now I could clearly see the shaitaans all around me. Along with this clarity came fear, sorrow and a strange happiness. Fear of living among shaitaans. Sorrow at growing up. And happiness at finally understanding Ammi's, precious advice and seeing a clear picture of the world around me.

Six

After witnessing thirty-five full moons, five rains and two heavy snowfalls.

It was one of those evenings when the sun had already set. I heard a *Sitti,* whistle– its sound carried fear and unease. By that time, Tahir had taught me how to whistle, and I had mastered it to the point that I could do it even with one finger. Whenever we ventured deep into the jungle and got separated, we used whistles to communicate. A thin, sharp *Sitti* meant, "where are you? Come back now!" whereas a loud *Sitti,* blown using two fingers from both hands, signified danger of fear. We often used the loud *Sitti* in the village whenever a leopard came by.

Tahir also taught me another thing– a secret tied to Subedar Dada's half opened eyes. It was *charas,* hashish. By rubbing *bhang,* cannabis leaves with both hands until a dark residue collected, Tahir would dry it and sell it to Dada and other hashish smokers in the village. In return, we got few coins, which we spent on buying *gachak* and other sweets. The cannabis jungle was little far from our village, but we frequently went there when

Ammi was not around. Tahir would shape the dried dark residue into tiny balls, resembling goat droppings, and later sell them.

That *Sitti,* whistle, was the danger whistle. I recognized it immediately, especially when it blew for the third time. I asked Ammi, who was cleaning *dheed,* fern for dinner. The moment the whistle sounded; an entire silence descended upon the village. Ammi grabbed my arm, pushed me onto Dayi's cot, and said, "Noor! Don't go outside without asking! just sit here quietly."

Then Ammi and Dayi went outside. After a while, they returned. The room was lit by *kunzalwan,* but they extinguished it, leaving us in silence and darkness. Bolting the door shut, shut they sat down together. My mind was filled with questions. Why is this happening? Is baba involved in something? Or is it Afzal again? Ammi usually locked the door only when she feared Afzal.

These thoughts echoed in my head until I heard foot-steps near the door, followed by loud banging. I was terrified. Ammi quickly covered my mouth with her hand and held me tightly against her chest. Dayi whispered something to Ammi, telling her to hide behind the wooden partition. Behind that partition was where Dayi kept her cattle.

Holding me in her arms, Ammi stumbled through the darkness, bumping into the wall, and laid us down near the *khurli,* cattle's feeding trough.

The noise at the door grew louder. Then I heard Dayi opened the door yell angrily. I couldn't see anything; I could only imagine the scene from the voices. There were three or four men. One of them demanded, "where is Hassan's *kanjri*? Tell us! she lives with you, doesn't she? We've heard she is close to the *kafirs.* Where are you hiding her, old hag? Is she the *muqbir,* whistleblower?"

I don't know for whom the word *kafir* was used, I couldn't understand their intension.

However, what Mulla Bashir-ul-Haq taught me and what Ammi taught me is that a *kafir* is someone who doesn't obey God, who doesn't follow His commands, someone who lies. Ammi used to say that those who take away someone's freedom, those who unjustly harm others, those who deprive someone of their rightful dues, and those who don't follow the rules set by God–they are the ones who can be called *kafirs.*

One of them hit Dayi, and I heard her cry out in pain. Another said, "old hag, we'll come every day. Let's see how long you can hide her. We'll tear you to pieces!"

Ammi kept my mouth covered. The fear was so overwhelming that I eventually fell asleep in her arms.

After that it became routine, by then we had three homes: Siyah Bakht for sleeping on normal days, Dayi's house for cooking and cattle house for sleeping during dangerous nights.

This pattern alternated. For few weeks, we would sleep peacefully in Siyah Bakht whenever the *fojis,* soldiers were stationed in our village. But during those times, men even boys, were subjected to torture, while the women found some relief. However, whenever the soldiers left, the night soldiers would arrive. They tortured everyone, especially women. During those nights, the men found some respite.

The soldiers would take men during the day, and the militants would take them at night, but it was the innocent women who bore the brunt of the torture from the night soldiers– militants.

Sometimes, I would question: Whose land is this? If it belonged to us, the villagers, why would the fojis torture us? If it belonged to the day soldiers why did the night soldiers come? This confusion always lingered in my mind, and by the time I understood it all, I had already left the village.

I had now left that place behind. The village where Ammi and Dayi had taught me all the philosophies of life. The things I couldn't comprehend while living in the village were now becoming clear to me after leaving it. Even those things that I had never tried to understand were now slowly starting to make sense.

For years, life had felt like a riddle with missing pieces. There were questions I dared not ask, truths I wasn't ready to face, and memories I didn't want to carry. Yet, slowly, it seemed as if the blurred outlines of my world were beginning to sharpen, revealing a picture I wasn't sure I wanted to see.

But was it? Truly?

An evening, after five days later, I sat quietly in the corner of Dayi's *chula*, staring at the flickering diya casting shadows on the cracked walls. The room felt smaller somehow, its silence pressing against me. Ammi was outside, preparing for the night, and I could hear the faint rustle of her movements, steady but cautious. Every sound carried a weight, a sense of impending danger, as if the air itself had learned to tread lightly in our village.

The *Sitti*—the sharp whistle that had signaled danger earlier—still echoed in my mind. It was Tahir who had taught me its meaning, how different sounds could speak without words.

I thought of Tahir, his mischievous grin and his endless energy. He had taught me so much—not just about whistles or the secret of Subedar Dada's hashish, but about the small joys that could be found even in a life as fraught as ours. I wondered where he was now, whether he was safe.

The door creaked open, and Ammi entered, her face lined with worry. She bolted the door behind her and set down the bundle of firewood she had been carrying. Her hands trembled slightly as she adjusted her dupatta, but her eyes, those cat-like eyes that mirrored my own, held their usual resolve.

"Noor," she said, her voice soft but firm, "tonight we stay inside. Don't open the door for anyone, not even Dayi, unless I tell you."

I nodded, though her words sent a shiver down my spine. Nights like these had become more frequent, and I had learned to recognize the signs—Ammi's tightened jaw, the extra logs she placed against the door, the way her hands hovered near the *chula* as if it could offer more than just warmth.

"Is it the shaitaans again?" I asked, my voice barely above a whisper. Ammi looked at me for a long moment, her expression unreadable. Then she knelt down beside me, brushing a strand of hair from my face. "Noor, sit by the fire and stay quiet. Everything will be alright."

Her words lingered in the air; I wasn't sure I wanted to understand. I thought of Baba, of Afzal, of the men who came at night and the ones who claimed to protect us during the day. Each one had taken something from us—our peace, our dignity, our hope.

That night, as the darkness settled over the village, the silence outside became deafening. Every creak of the wooden beams, every rustle of the wind, seemed magnified. Ammi sat by the door, her back straight, her hands clutching a small stick she had picked up from the courtyard. It was a feeble weapon, but in her hands, it looked like a symbol of defiance. I lay on the *charpai,* pretending to sleep but unable to close my eyes. My mind raced with thoughts of the past—the moments of fleeting joy with Tahir, the nights spent hiding in Dayi's house, the whispers of stories Ammi would tell me to make sense of a world that often felt senseless.

And then there were the questions. Why did the fojis beat our men if they were here to protect us? Why did the militants hurt our women if they claimed to fight for freedom? And most of all, why did Baba and Afzal hate us so much when we had done nothing to deserve it?

Ammi's voice broke through my thoughts, low and steady. "Noor, do you know what it means to be free?"

I turned to her, startled by the question. "It means... to not be scared, I think."

She smiled faintly, though her eyes remained distant. "Freedom, Jigar, is not just the absence of fear. It is the right to live without chains—the ones others put on you and the ones you place on yourself. It is the ability to dream without guilt, to love without shame, to speak without fear of silencing. Remember this, Noor. No one can take your freedom unless you let them." Her words stayed with me long after she had fallen asleep, her body curled against the door as if to shield me from whatever lay outside.

The next morning, the village was abuzz with rumors of another raid. Some said the militants had clashed with the fojis in the neighboring valley; others whispered of betrayals and disappearances. Afzal's name was mentioned more than once, his shadowy dealings with the night soldiers no longer a secret.

By midday, a group of soldiers arrived, their faces grim, their voices sharp as they questioned the villagers. I watched from behind the *roshandan* as they interrogated Baba, their words barely audible over the pounding of my heart. For a moment, I felt a flicker of hope that they might take him away, that we might finally be free of his cruelty. But he returned, his face twisted with anger, his eyes searching for something—or someone—to punish.

As the days passed, the tension in the village grew thicker, like a storm gathering strength. The pieces of the puzzle were starting to fall into place, but the picture they formed was one of loss, fear, and survival. And yet, amidst the chaos, a seed of understanding began to grow within me. Perhaps freedom was not something you waited for. Perhaps it was something you created, one small act of courage at a time.

Seven

1973- in the month of *Shravan*, everywhere, all around there was greenery– lush and endless. Yet, for me, it felt no different than a dark black jungle. I couldn't see any colors, though the *khoobani,* apricot trees were indeed flowering.

One day, Ammi and I were heading to the forest to gather dry firewood and *kunzalwan*. Just as we left the village, we passed by the last house, which belonged to Sakina Aapi. She was Ammi's friend and often accompanied her to the forest, where they'd spend hours talking. Outside her house stood a sturdy *khoobani* tree, with thick golden *khoobani* just like the scarf which I wore. She would sell most of them but always kept some aside for us, and never once scolded me when I'd grab a few.

As we walked past, I picked one of the apricot's golden white flowers, holding it tenderly in my hand as we moved on. A little way down the path, near the stone by the bend, we sat down to rest, that's when Ammi turned to me, her eyes warm, and said, "Noor Jigar, do you know what the biggest *gunah,* sin in the world is?"

Curious, I looked at her, eager to understand her words. "The biggest sin, "she continued, "is when you strip someone of their freedom. Look Noor, you plucked the flower. You took its life. You snatched away its freedom, its right to live and grow. It would have blossomed into a delicious *khoobani*. I couldn't fully grasp her meaning, but I watched her slight bright lips move and curve of a smile, and her *shahadat* finger, raising as if pointing directly at me while she spoke.

She laughed softly, "Noor Jigar, do you even understand what I'm saying?" I just nodded, offering her a smile in return.

Today, there were those same flowers, but the moment was different. Ammi had truly left her Noor and gone to sleep, forever, with the angels in the graveyard.

I sat on the same corner of our *aangan* from where the path turns to other houses, questioning myself over and over, wondering if it was my fault. Maybe, one day, I had disobeyed Ammi's words and taken *gachak*, a kind of sweet made by mixing jaggery with groundnut, from Afzal's hand. Was it because of me that Ammi had gone to sleep?

Sitting in the corner of *aangan* dressed in white *poshak* that Dayi had made me wear. Ammi, too was lying on a cot, wrapped in similar white sheet. The village women came one by one to Ammi, weeping uncontrollably, and then to me.

Ammi lay still under the white sheet, and there were water stains on it– the same stains she had once mentioned while dressing me, the same *poshak* bought from *bazaar*, market.

I had heard the name of *bazaa*r countless times from Subedar Dada. Every time I asked him, "Dada, where do you get things when they run out?" he'd say, "Noori, from the bazaar," laughing as he spoke. "How many times will you ask, my Noor! One day, I'll take you to the bazaar and leave you there."

The bazaar was somewhere down the hills, far enough that it couldn't be seen.

Once, Ammi gave her black goat to Subedar Dada for his son's Ajmal Mama's wedding, "Ammi told me that he is your Mama, the maternal uncle, so I used to call him Ajmal Mama." Perhaps, in return, Dada took us to the bazaar.

Few days after the wedding one *Sumwar,* Monday morning, early at dawn, Ammi got ready. She wore white jutti, the same kind Parveen had worn on her wedding day, covered her face with a black *rumal,* handkerchief, dressed me in my lush green kurta, and took me to Dada's shop as the first rays of the sun began peeking through the eastern deodar trees.

When we reached the shop, Ammi greeted, "Salam, Abaji." She used to call Dada Abaji. Dada's voice was deep and heavy, though half of it seemed to disappear into the thick, curved mustache. He quickly began packing up the shop and locked its plain deodar wood door before slinging a *jhola*– bag over his shoulder.

We started walking down the hills towards the bazaar, I was thrilled. The bazaar I had always heard about existed only in my imagination– a long village filled with endless sweets, food, clothes, bangles, and earrings.

In my excitement, I began counting my steps. By then, Ammi had already taught me to write and read numbers up to *hazar*– thousand, as well as to read and write Urdu all on a slate– just a plain piece of rock. Ammi never refused to teach me anything, as if she knew everything. She often told me stories of the Turks, Razia Sultana, Rani Jhansi, Zulaikha, Zulkarnain and during wars about Chinese and Mongols.

As we moved closer to the *bazaar*, I kept watching our shadows– Dada leading, Ammi and me following. I counted *saat soo unchass*– seven hundred forty-nine steps before I stopped. Dada then lifted me onto his shoulders and with a deep, broad voice said, "Noor, come on! Ride on Dada's shoulders," followed by a hearty laugh, "Ha ha ha!"

Besides Ammi Subedar Dada was the only other person who had ever carried me on his shoulders. From up there, I could see an amazing view. After walking for a while, I held Ammi's hand again. I noticed our shadows were getting smaller. Ammi explained to me that it was probably *Zohar*– afternoon prayer time. When the shadow becomes small, it is *Zohar* time, she had said.

We were nearing the *bazaar*. The noise and bustle were growing, just like the chaos we'd experience during Eid or weddings back in our village. Ahead I saw a horse pulling a wooden cart with two wheels. It carried sacks and some goods, just like the ones Ammi had drawn on the slate for me, except she hadn't drawn the bearded man driving it.

Slowly, I started understanding that it was where Dada got the goods for his shop. Ammi leaned close to me and whispered, "Noor! This is *Tay-Tonga*," referring to what she had once taught me in Urdu.

We were now close to the bazaar, and it was nothing like I had imagined. There was noise, movement, crowds– men and women walking together. Some women wore burqa, while others didn't. Some held hands, walking in sync with others. And then there was trash– plastic bags scattered here and there. Back in our village, even near Dada's shop, there was some litter, but not like this.

The bazaar had all kind of shops– overflowing with clothes, earrings and bangles. We entered one of the shops, and Ammi bought me white *poshak*, a *pheran,* and a new pair of white jutti. Dada bought bangles and scarf. Ammi also got me a nose pin and said, "Noor this year Sakina Aapi will pierce your nose, and then you'll wear this pin."

I remembered when I had my ears pierced. I was sitting in Ammi's lap, and it was winter. After the piercing, Ammi had promised to buy me *gachak* in return.

As we left the bazaar, I saw a large group of children with wooden slates in their hands and *jhola* on their backs. All were wearing similar clothes– green pajama like trousers and white shirts. Curious, I asked Ammi, "who are they? Why are they wearing same clothes?"

"These are school children, just like you go to Mulla to learn Arabic, they come here to learn Urdu too" Ammi replied.

I asked, "Ammi, did you also learn here? Because you always have answers to everything."

"Nah, Jigar. Hurry up! Dada has gone ahead; we must catch up."

Today, I was wearing that white *poshak.* For the first time, I saw Baba standing near Ammi. My eyes searched for Parveen. She was standing near Siyah Bakht room, but she wasn't crying. Maybe she was angry with Baba, who stood over the *charpai.*

In the corner of the *aangan* they bathed Ammi– not in our *Gusal khana,* but in an area covered with sheets on all sides, even from above. Unlike our open-to-sky bathroom, this setup was different. Perhaps the water stains came from here.

The stains I remembered one time when Ammi was dressing me in the white *poshak,* she had said,

"Noor! Jigar, females like you, me and everyone are just like your white poshak. See these water stains from your wet hair on your dress? Just like that women are like white garments– they bear every stain."

As always, I listened with my eyes closed. Ammi asked again, "Noor! Are you listening?"

I kissed her hand– the same hand that was on my shoulder as she helped me dress– and smiled at her.

At the bend of the path, I saw Mulla Bashir-ul-Haq approaching. The noise and crowd grew louder. Amidst the chaos, someone grabbed my arm and led me to Dayi, who stood near Ammi.

"*Alwida deedar*," farewell sight, someone said, as Dayi removed the white sheet covering Ammi's face. She was lying there, still, her face as pale as her shroud, except for the faint bluish mark– the kind Baba sometimes left on her face. I kissed her forehead and cheeks. She was as cold as ice. Leaning close to her ear, I whispered, "don't worry. I'll listen to everything you said, but wake up soon."

The mark on her face had been there for three days. Three days ago, on a *Jumah*– Friday, Ammi had dropped me off at Sakina Aapi's house before going with her to collect leaves from the tree. Shortly after, Sakina Aapi was supporting Ammi, by her shoulders, helping her walk. Since then, Ammi had not moved.

Over these three days, she hadn't gone anywhere. I would bring her two chapattis made with turmeric and medicinal herbs from Dayi's house and fetch her water.

At night, I would sleep with my legs nestled between Ammi's legs and her soft arms encircling me. Ammi didn't hum the usual lullaby. Instead, she spoke in a voice filled with pain, as if she were aching deeply.

"Noor, if I sleep forever, go to Dayi's house. She will take care of you. Don't ever come to this room. Stay away from every shaitaan, maybe she meant people like Afzal."

The men moved to one side, and the women to the other. Mulla Bashir at the front, leading the prayer as Ammi lay there.

Subedar Dada, Mulla, Gafar Chacha, Rehmat Chacha lifted the *charpai* by its four corners and began walking towards the graveyard. The women were left behind in the *aangan*. I was watching the entire scene from the corner of our *aangan*.

Perhaps a question lingered in my heart: if everyone goes to sleep in the *kabristan*– graveyard, why doesn't anyone rise again? Maybe I had started to believe that this was the last time I would see Ammi. My eyes burst into warm tears running down my cheeks. The path ahead some blurry. I didn't even realize when I started running towards the *kabristan,* and there; I saw Ammi being hidden beneath the soil for the last time.

Eight

It was the month of *Asshar*– the peak of summer. Villagers were busy cutting grass immersed in the chores. But for me, every single day stretched into eternity. But for me, every single day stretched into eternity. Every season felt bland, as if time itself had lost its color.

It was third *Asshar* that two years, twelve days, three hundred forty-one visible moonlit nights, eight heavy downpours, three snowfalls since Ammi's passing. Every day I would sneak to her grave and pour my heart out to her, sharing secrets only she could keep. My only companion now was Dayi Ammi, and sometimes Tahir, who managed to lift my spirits with his childish antics.

One day, I was taking our goats to graze in the nearby fields. Tahir tagged along with his cattle. On our way we noticed Afzal walking up the hill, carrying a heavy sack on his shoulder. His eyes met mine, and he yelled at the top of his voice,

"Stop, you daughter of wretched woman!"

I ignored him but his voice grew louder and harsher.

"Your mother was a *kanjri,* a disgrace, and you're no different–following in her footsteps! How many fathers do you have? Huh, tell me? Your two-colored eyes reveal everything."

He said and then laughed loudly.

I didn't respond and spat on the ground, then placed my foot on it. This is what Ammi used to say: "whenever you see shaitaan or evil, do the same thing. Lower your gaze and change your position." She also used to say that shaitaan like, Shephard's purse *(capsella bursa)* – a weed thorn that sticks to the clothes, so the farther you stay, the safer you'll be.

Tahir, ever protective, couldn't hold back. He smirked sarcastically.

"Well, well, Rasheed's son. What's gotten into you today?"

Afzal always taunted Tahir about Rasheed, a villager who frequently visited Tahir's home to buy dried vegetables, implying some scandalous connection.

Afzal spat back, "and you, filthy daughter of a disgrace!"

Before I could react, Tahir's temper flared. He charged at Afzal and shoved him hard, causing the sack to fall off his shoulder. Afzal retaliated by grabbing Tahir's arm and shoving him into the dusty path, where the loose dirt coated half of Tahir's face and teeth. He looked a mess, with dirt streaked across his face and his dignity bruised.

Afzal wasn't done. He grabbed the back of Tahir's kameez and ripped it apart. Then, glaring at me with venom in his eyes, he sneered,

"Go on, enjoy the sigh of your *harami* soulmate now!"

Tahir, struggled to stand, turned to me, his voice hoarse and broken. "Nool, you go... just go. I'll handle this *khanzeer*– pig myself."

I hesitated but obeyed, my heart heavy with worry. I asked myself; did I do the wrong thing by running away? Did I make a mistake by leaving Tahir alone?

I remembered a time when a foji, had caught Tahir and tried to intimidate him. I had stood by his side, holding onto his arm, giving him courage to face the situation. After questioning us, the soldier handed us a small packet of sweets. We had shared it between us, but Tahir, as always, gave me a little more than his own share. Perhaps he had no other close friends, or maybe he just wanted to see me happy.

Was I making mistake now by abandoning him? Later, Tahir appeared, his face was wearing an expression I had never seen before– sadness. It was the first time I saw the ever-cheerful Tahir without a smile.

I tried asking him repeatedly why he was upset, but he deflected my questions every time, steering the conversation elsewhere.

That day, I understand what Ammi used to say: on the day of *Qayamat*– judgement, your intentions and heart will be judged, for only God knows what lies within.

I thought I knew Tahir well, but I couldn't grasp the storm brewing inside him. The person who bought joy to everyone's lives carried a burden no one could see. How much Ammi must have concealed in her own heart, I wondered.

For weeks, Tahir was unusually silent, and his smile never returned. That was also the last time I saw him by my side grazing cattle and goats.

Exactly *tertalis*– forty-three days later, I spotted Tahir in a crowd. He was wearing the same black salwar kameez, the very outfit Ammi had bought for Tahir and me. I had worn mine several times, but Tahir had worn his only once– on a Friday when I had teased him, saying, "you look like a *Peer*– saint in these clothes."

That day, I was veiled, my face hidden behind the mesh of my burqa. Through the thin screen, I saw a face in the crowd– Tahir's. His usual mischievous grin was replaced by a deep sorrow. It felt like he had, just like Ammi, taught me an invaluable lesson: nothing in this world is permanent. Everything is fleeting.

As I stood in the crowd, someone gently grabbed my arm, placed my hand in Saleem Lala's, and said, "come, it's time for your *rukhsati*– final farewell."

We began descending the village path. Saleem Lala walked ahead while I followed, my heart heavy with unspoken words. A storm of tears welled up inside me. I kept turning back, looking at every curve in the path. At each turn, I saw Tahir standing there, waving his white shawl– a gesture we often used to say goodbye.

Perhaps that innocent gesture contained all the unspoken emotions that no one else could see or understand. Some things are beyond human perception. If our eyes could see everything, we would glimpse the shaitaan in some and divine in other.

That day, I walked away, but I left a piece of my soul behind with Tahir and memories of Ammi and Dayi.

Saleem was a merchant whose business was to transport goods from one place to another. He had no permanent home. He was an orphan and shared a good acquaintance with Subedar Dada.

It had been twenty-seven days since Dayi Ammi passed away.

One day, I went to fetch water from the spring with a small earthen pot. It was evening, the time of *Asar* prayers, and the sun was on the verge of setting, casting an orange glow across the sky. As I returned, descending the slope towards our house, I noticed a crowd gathered outside Dayi's home. My steps quickened, an unease building within me. Reaching her doorway, I hastily placed the pot on the ground and rushed inside.

There on the *charpai,* Dayi Ammi lay still, while three-four women from the village were covering her with a white shroud. A wave of darkness enveloped my vision. Today the second *bunyaad* of my life, after Ammi, was leaving me forever. She was going to rest in the graveyard. I felt my legs weaken, and I lost consciousness.

Memories began flooding back– how Dayi had become my strength after Ammi passed away. She nurtured me, raised me, took care of me when I was at my weakest. I recalled a particular day vividly. She was sitting on her *charpai,* braiding my hair with colorful threads. I had asked her in trembling voice,

"Dayi, will you also leave me one day, like Ammi did?"

She gently patted my head and said lovingly, "Noor, Jigar every living being has to face death one day. No one stays forever. Everyone leaves some as devils and some as divine souls." As she spoke her words carried the usual smell of *naswar,* and her voice, as always, was raspy from her age.

Suddenly, Dayi had stood up and said, "stay here, I have something to give you." She pulled up her loose kameez, revealing another layer underneath with deep pockets sewn into it. She reached into one of the pockets and took out a polythene tied with several knots. Inside it were a few coins and a small bundle of things wrapped carefully. Then, she bought out a pouch and handed it to me, saying, "take your *amanat*– trust."

I opened the pouch with trembling hands, and inside was a small nose pin– one I immediately recognized, the same nose pin Ammi had bought from *bazaar* during one of our trips with Subedar Dada. My heart tightened.

"Dayi, how did you get this?" I, asked barely able to form the words.

Dayi's tired eyes softened as she replied, "Maryam gave it to me when she was unwell. She told me 'When Noor grows up, make her wear it."

And now, though nose pin was with me, Dayi was not. As the sun set the evening, taking the light of day with it, Dayi too had set forever, taking a piece of my heart along with her.

A day, when I was at Dayi's house, smearing lay on the *Chula* in preparation for Eid. Subedar Dada was coming down the street with a few men, I ran to *aangan* to peek. Subedar Dada went straight to Baba's house while the men stayed outside. As I continued my work, Dada knocked on the door. I stepped out, he handed me a sealed package.

"Noori, quickly get ready," he said handling over the package having a picture of beautiful girl with blood red, flowing hair, wearing the same crimson, maroon-colored fabric as in the package. Without a second thought, I started preparing myself.

After I was ready, I saw Parveen approach me for the first time. She said, "come Hassan is calling."

I felt a wave of fear and uneasiness. Questions swirled in my head. "Why? What do they want?" I reassured myself, thinking, Subedar Dada is here; nothing bad can happen.

When I went downstairs from Dayi's house to *Siyah Bakht* room, I took the same path where Ammi and I used to sit on the stone after dinner, gazing at the moon together, and then, on the slate-like stone in front of us, she would draw a line to count the visible moons.

Parveen led me into room, handed me a burqa and a pair of white shoes adorned with shimmering little sequins, delicately stitched with fine threads. I wore the burqa and sat down, the scene reminded me of the day Ammi sat in the same room, sobbing bitterly when Baba bought Parveen home. There was a joy outside but mourning within us.

Those memories came alive as if playing before my eyes– a surreal, haunting illusion. The room's familiarity only deepened my anguish, making me feel as though history was repeating itself. Could it be the memories and the setting were the same, only the people had changed? Lost in thought, I noticed my trembling hands. I glanced at the *roshandan,* and an overwhelming sense of dread filled me– fear of loneliness, fear of shaitaans, fear of the unknown.

Before I could gather myself, footsteps approached the door. A group of three-four people entered. My face was covered with burqa's mesh veil, but through it, I recognize Afzal, a stranger,

Mulla Bashir-ul-Haq, Baba and Subedar Dada. My mind was in turmoil. "Why is Mulla here? Why Afzal? Why Dada? Who is this stranger?"

Parveen came and sat beside me, holding my arm. Mulla Bashir began reciting something in Arabic, followed by few supplications, some of which I remembered, while others were unfamiliar. Then he asked the stranger, *"Qabool?"* the stranger in a deep voice replied thrice, *"Qabool, Qabool, Qabool."*

The same question was directed at me. I stayed silent, my heart racing as I recalled Ammi correcting Tahir and me when we pretended to marry the *Roon Wangun,* (oak tree seeds). She had told us, "A Mulla makes you say *Qabool* three times during a wedding." As always, my supplementary question. "What if one of them refuses?" Ammi smiled and said, "Noor, you will understand on your own and smiled."

Now I understood the reality of what was happening. I remained quiet. Parveen pinched my arm forcefully, urging to respond but I still said nothing. Subedar Dada intervened, saying loudly, "Saleem Sahib, don't worry. She's just nervous." The mention of Saleem's name confirmed my fears. He was stranger because there was no one by that name in our village.

Mulla repeated, "Noor! Do you accept this *nikah* with Saleem? Say *Qabool* three times."

Parveen pinched me again, harder this time, as if to compel me to speak. I nodded thrice silently. Everyone seemed pleased. Then I heard Baba's voice instructing, "come outside to the *aangan*; I have arranged for food."

Everyone left for *aangan*. Baba stayed behind, seemingly hesitant to approach me. Eventually, he came closer, and I instinctively moved back, scared. Baba stopped and for the first time, called me by my name,

"Noor, placing his hand on my head. His voice held something I couldn't understand.

I never hated Baba, but yes, I had witnessed the torture he inflicted on Ammi, which turned him into a shaitaan in my eyes. Now the situation was different. There was a lot of resentment in my heart, but there was also a flicker of hope that maybe Baba would apologize and say to me, "Noor, I never treated you like a daughter. Forgive me."

I remember, whenever I asked Ammi, "Baba hurts you, why don't you leave him and live somewhere else?" She would reply, "Noor, when you will grow up, you will understand on your own. Where there are emotions, whether the *bunyaad* is strong or weak, expectations always arise."

I was beginning to understand why I was expecting these things from Baba. Even though he had always tortured us, committed injustices, these things from Baba. Even though he had always tortured us, committed injustices, there was a part of me that hoped– maybe he would cry, maybe he would realize his mistake.

Just then, Parveen's son, Iqbal came to call Baba, and he walked out of the room.

I was left alone, enveloped in an overwhelming silence. A silence mourning Ammi's absence, Dayi's absence, every person I had ever been close to. The silence of the village's walls, its lively streets, and the cheerful weather. The silence of every morning and every evening. The silence of days and nights spent in this room.

This moment felt like a crossroads– one step into an unknown future and another in painful past. It reminded me of old *khaw* tree, where Tahir had once built a swing in the fields. We used to place our feet on two branches, each swaying in different direction– just like this situation, pulling me into opposing worlds, one with uncertain future, the other with lingering sorrow. I was lost, confused, and powerless against the tide of emotions pulling me in every direction.

I was in *Siyah Bakht* while the rest of the people were outside, enjoying the feast. Iqbal entered the room and placed a plate of food in front of me. This scene only deepened the wounds of the past, making them fresh again. I didn't touch a single morsel.

Meanwhile, the noise and chatter outside grew louder. Everyone stood up as Parveen entered the room and said, "get ready quickly; it's time for your *rukhsati*– the final farewell."

Hearing this a spark ignited within me. It dawned me on that this might be my final moment in this room. I quickly stood up and walked to the corner of the room, where an old wooden shelf stood. On it lay a hand-knitted cap with my name embroidered by Ammi with her own hands. I picked it up and returned to my place.

In no time, a few women from the village, along with Parveen, led me out of the room. The men stood at the far end of the *aangan*, near the path leading out of the village. They moved forward as Parveen walked me to the center of the *aangan.* I couldn't see anything; my eyes were blurred with memories. All I could make out were the boots and chappals of people in the *aangan* around me.

Amidst the commotion, I suddenly heard someone calling "Noor!" I recognized the voice– it was Shabana Baji. She approached me, grabbed my arm, and led me to a corner of the *aangan*. Leaning close to my ear, she whispered softly, "Noor! You are free now. Leave this cursed village and live your freedom to the fullest."

She handed me a ring she always used to wear, marking my *rukhsati*. I stood there confused, by this so-called freedom. Was this the freedom Ammi used to talk about? She would always say, "one must never take away someone's freedom," like the time I plucked a blossomed *khoobani* flower.

But now, I couldn't understand– was my freedom being taken away, or was I being set free? Caught in this turmoil of thought, my mind grew heavy, and my eyes filled with tears of grief.

As soon as we left the village a little distance behind, I saw Subedar Dada following us. My steps froze abruptly, and I was lost in whirlwind of thoughts– what if Dada takes me back? What if he changes his mind? I wished desperately that Dada would call me back, that he would stop me and take me home.

We were nearing Dada's shop, the spot where the path led to the market-place. Dada reached us. He asked Saleem to stop at the shop for a moment. I was in burqa with netted veil over my eyes, allowing me to see everything– the wooden radio pole outside Dada's shop, his hurried movements as he unlocked the shop and began packing something into polythene bag. Saleem in the meantime pulled out a stubby bidi from his pocket, lit it, and began smoking. My gaze remained fixed on Dada, waiting for him to call me, and hold my hand and say, "Noor! Let's go back home." But these were just my thoughts, my hopes. Tears blurred my vision.

Dada approached me, held me by my arm, and led me a little away from Saleem, near the radio pole. Dada's eyes were fully open, perhaps Dada hadn't smoked hashish. He handed me the polythene bag and, in a voice, that felt wilted, said softly, "Noor, this village is no longer yours. Saleem is a good man; I have known him for fifteen years. He will keep you happy." His words confused me. Why was he saying this? Then, joining his hands, Dada said, "Noor, don't come back to this village alone again."

I stood stunned. What did he mean? Why was he speaking to me this way? I couldn't find the courage to respond. My silence was heavy with questions. Dada placed his hand on my head and gave me a gentle shake. "Noor, I need a promise from you. Swear to me that you won't return to this village alone."

What could I say? Why should I promise? How could I? There was mourning inside me, a silence so loud it had choked my voice. I simply nodded. Dada turned and entered his shop, without once looking back at me. His retreating figure left me with more unanswered questions than I could articulate.

From inside, I heard in voice, "Saleem, *Khuda Hafiz.* Leave quickly. The *manzil*– destination is far."

What was this *manzil?* Was it the same *manzil* Ammi reached while living with Baba? Or was it the eternal sleep of a graveyard?

Saleem began walking ahead. Though the netted veil, I saw his left hand resting on his back, a thick silver ring with a black shiny stone on his *shahadat* finger and a bidi burning in his other hand. I followed him silently.

Suddenly, a faint *Sitti* caught my attention. I turned around abruptly. At the curve of the village path, where we used to rest often, stood a large stone. On that stone, I had once written "Noor" in Urdu. I remember when I was writing the name; Ammi and I had just fetched water from the spring. Ammi scolded me gently, then crooked a playful smile, just like the way she used to smile and said, "Noor, I didn't educate you to crave your name on stones; I taught you to understand life." She paused then added with a chuckle, "Go ahead, write your name. The *Rantas* will call you by this very name in the silence of the night."

Standing on the stone, draped in a black salwar kameez and weaving a white shawl, was Tahir. Maybe this was his final goodbye.

I lifted my hand instinctively to whistle back, but before I could, Saleem said, "They are *Bakarwals;* keep walking. The *manzil* is far."

I stopped and turned back, walking behind Saleem once again. This time I wasn't counting my steps. Instead, every step bought more questions– Why did Dada say that to me? Why am I leaving the Kahsar Pur? Why is it always women who must leave their homes, not the men?

After walking some time, exhaustion overtook me, but I said nothing. The sharp edge of my shoe's heel was biting into my foot. My foot was wounded, each step bringing pain, though it was nothing compared to the ache inside me.

The shadows of our body began to shorten as the sun climbed higher. It was noon. Saleem stopped abruptly and sat down, clearly tired. I stood still, and he gestured for me to sit. I lowered myself to the ground, finally noticing my foot. The skin of my heel had peeled off, and blood was dripping. I took off my shoe. Saleem rose again and resumed walking. I picked up my shoes, carrying them in my hand, and began walking barefoot, the harsh earth below a small relief from the storm brewing inside me.

While walking I saw a man carrying his daughter on his shoulders, with his wife following closely behind. Abruptly, I began to see myself in them. The little girl on his shoulders wasn't there anymore; she had turned into the woman walking behind him. That woman was now me.

After walking a little further, we neared *bazaar.* Saleem approached a Tonga driver standing nearby and spoke with him for a while. He then gestured for me to come closer. Barefoot and hesitant, I made my way toward him. He signaled with his finger for me to sit on Tonga. I climbed in, put my shoes back on, and looked at the scene unfolding behind me.

Through the mesh of my veil, I saw the world I was leaving behind– my childhood, my memories– all slipping further away. As the Tonga moved forward, the trees, stones and everything I had grown up with faded into the distance, just like my village, just like my past.

Nine

1976- it had been seventeen suffocating days, and yet again, an incident occurred. The night was just as dark, the air just as heavy. Seventeen days had passed since I found myself utterly alone. I had arrived at this place exhausted from the journey, but Shobha Boba– the landlord, had taken me in.

Shobha Boba lived alone in the ground floor of her house. The people upstairs called her *Panditayan.* I used to call her Boba. She had a striking appearance– her hair was a mix of black and grey, and her teeth often bore the faint stains of *Jhajri* smoke. She always adorned a bright red bindi on her forehead, giving her sense of dignity amidst her solitude. She was the widow of a man killed in crossfire, Shobha Boba was not sure whether it was militant's bullet or soldiers. Her only son worked far away in another city much like Saleem. Her primary source of income seemed to be cooking for the tenants of her house, and this included Saleem, who she cared for like a son.

It didn't take long for us to develop a bond. I often helped in her kitchen. She taught me how to cook with a motherly affection and would always marvel at my eyes, calling me unique, as though I was someone destined for great things. She would say, "your mother must be an extraordinary woman to have birthed a daughter like you."

During those seventeen days, I spent my time reading an Urdu newspaper that lay on Saleem's desk. It bore the word *Ranbir* in bold black ink. I read it from line to line each day, filling the hours with its stories. In the afternoons, I would cook with Shobha Boba, and from *Asar* to *Maghrib*, I would immerse myself in the same newspaper.

That night was different. I had just finished dinner and was lying in a corner of the room when I heard the sound of footsteps on the wooden stairs. There was a knock at the door. My heart raced. I hesitated, but then I heard Saleem's voice from the other side, asking me to open the door. I unlocked it with trembling hands, and he walked in wearing a long jacket and boots. Without a word he strode to the chair by the desk and sat down, gesturing for me to light the lamp.

I did as he said, the flickering light casting shadows across the room. He put his feet up on the table and motioned for me to remove his boots. I hesitated, but his voice deep and commanding, left no room for defiance. As I knelt to remove his boots, a faint smell, musty and unwashed, wafted up. Then I peeled off his socks. He lit a thick bidi and exhaled clouds of smoke, his piercing gaze fixed on me.

As I tried to retreat, he barked, "press my legs!" I froze. My hands shook as I moved to comply, kneading his legs with hesitation. "Harder!" he demanded, his voice cutting through the air like a whip. My eyes darted up to his face– his beard was neatly trimmed, his mustache perfectly shaped. He seemed older, perhaps Afzal's age. After a while, he pointed toward the bed and said in commanding tone, "go lie down. I'll turn off the light."

I obeyed without question, retreating to the edge of the bed and covering myself with a sheet. Saleem extinguished the lamp, the room plunged into darkness. The bed cracked under his weight as he in. He pulled me toward him, and I felt its heavy, muscular frame shift the entire bed. My breath came in short, shallow gasps as fear gripped me. He turned me onto my back and began to touch me under my kameez.

It reminded me of the village– the horror I thought I had left behind.

After Dayi passed away, I was alone one evening, cooking dinner at her house. Three was a knock at the door. When I opened it, I saw group of *mujahids,* and among them was Afzal. They walked in without invitation, taking seats on Dayi's *charpai* as though it belonged to them, perhaps the leader, asked Afzal, "is this the girl?"

Afzal nodded and said, "yes, she's the one. I have promised her to Sulaiman."

Sulaiman was a young man in their group. They embraced each other, laughing and speaking in low voices.

Then, one of them grabbed my arm roughly and said, "if you so much as utter a sound, we'll fill you with bullets right here."

I was dragged to Shabana Baji's house under the cover of darkness. When Shabana Baji saw me, she let out a cry, her voice trembling with anguish. "You, beasts! You didn't even spare this *masoom*– innocent girl!" She turned to Afzal and screamed, "Afzal, may Allah destroy you! May you all perish!"

Her words were met with violence. One of the men struck her hard across the face, sending her crashing into the wall. Blood trickled down her cheek as she slumped to the ground, her spirit unbroken. They began eating their meal, laughing and talking as though nothing had happened. Sulaiman, the one I had been promised to, pulled me on to the *charpai* in the corner. His hands roamed under my kameez as he whispered, "you have now turned into fiery young beauty."

Shabana Baji must have been watching. Gathering her courage, she approached the men, bowing and pleading. "Do whatever you want with me. Kill me if you must. But leave this innocent girl alone."

Her pleas were met with scorn. The leader kicked her hard and snarled,

"Her mother was an informer; she will become too. Both of you belong to us, not the soldiers. Now get lost! But this isn't over. We will deal with you both later."

"Get lost! Shabana! You have become bland, undesirable woman," one of them sneered, and everyone burst into laughter.

Without hesitation, Shabana Baji grabbed my arm and dragged me out of the house. She ran, pulling me along the village's narrow paths under the faint light of the moon. Her voice broke as she repeated, "you can't stay here Noor. Not tonight."

We didn't stop until we reached Subedar Dada's house, far from the village. Shabana Baji knocked frantically until Dada opened the door, alarmed by urgency. She pushed me toward him, folding her hands in desperation. “This is an *amanat*– safekeeping. Protect her. The beasts had taken her...”

Tears streamed down her face as she spoke, her voice trembling with the weight of what had just happened.

That night we both stayed at Dada’s house. She tried to calm me down and offered me support. I had fainted out of fear. She said, “I am here, Dada is here. Don’t worry, we won’t leave you alone. From today, you will live here with Dada.”

After that day, Dada’s house became my place to sleep at night, and during the day, I would go to Dayi’s house to take care of our goats. The very next day Dada, called someone over the house and had conversation with them. It seemed that because of this conversation, I was here today.

Saleem, without a word, lifted my kameez, his movements deliberate, his touch invasive. The coarse hair on his chest and stomach brushed against my skin, sharp and unsettling, sending a shiver through me that wasn’t entirely fear– but it wasn’t comfort either. His face pressed closed to my neck, so close I could feel the roughness of his breath rasping against my skin, each exhale heavy, uneven and disturbingly intimate. The weight of his body bore down on me, unyielding, suffocating, like a mountain I couldn't escape.

His hand covered my mouth– a silencing gesture, more for himself than for me, as if he couldn't bear the possibility of my protest. After a moment, it was over. He exhaled deeply, turned his back to me, and fall asleep without a word, his body sprawled heavily beside mine.

I lay there for a moment, frozen in the remnants of his presence, the room still heavy with the scent of his sweat and the echo of his breath. Slowly, I pulled myself together, adjusting my clothes with trembling hands. Turning to the corner of the bed, I curled up tightly, facing away from him, and forced my eyes shut, willing sleep to find me.

After that this routine continued– a silent understanding that neither of us spoke of.

Sometimes it happened on alternate days, sometimes weeks would go by. At first, I felt confused, unsure whether it was something I needed. There were moments when his presence felt overbearing, intrusive even, but other times, it felt like a strange kind of closeness– a connection I couldn't define.

It became part of my nights, a rhythm I didn't entirely reject but didn't fully accept either, leaving me suspended in a space between discomfort and reluctant submission.

The submission didn't come all at once; it crept in slowly, like a shadow stretching as the day fades. I started to anticipate his movements, preparing myself for when his touch would demand my stillness. It became easier of to let go of resistance, to the weight of him press me into the mattress while my mind floated elsewhere, seeking refuge in the corner of my thoughts. And yet in the quiet moments after he would turn away, his breathing soft and steady in sleep. I would feel a strange emptiness settle over me. It wasn't pain, nor anger– it was something, quieter, something I couldn't quite name. I would pull my clothes back into place, turn toward the corner of the bed, and close my eyes, convincing myself that sleep would make it all disappear.

I began to tell myself that this, too, was a form of closeness– a twisted, unspoken bond that neither of us dared to acknowledge.

Ten

The bazaar buzzed with its usual life– the cacophony of vendors shouting prices, the vibrant displays of fresh vegetables, fruits and other goods stacked high on carts, even female undergarments were being sold openly. In Kahsar Pur, they were available at Dada's shop too, but they were always kept in a corner behind a curtain. Here, everything was in plain sight. It was bit surprising for me.

"Shobha Boba, teasing me with a smile, said, 'you want to buy? No, Saleem will buy it himself.' Then she smiled."

Shobha Boba and I had to come to buy some kitchen supplies. The market, just a few steps away from her house, was a narrow stretch of chaos bordered by carts on either side of the road.

The sun was climbing higher, its warm rays beginning to intensify as the day wore on. Vendors competed to outshot one another, calling customers with exaggerated gestures and loud declarations of their prices. The smell of freshly cut greens mingled with the musty scent of old wooden carts and the occasional whiff of tobacco.

Shobha Boba led the way, confidently navigating the crowd. I followed her closely, my eyes scanning the colorful chaos. Ever since I started living at her house, we had developed a close bond. She was my confidante, my guide in this new world.

Shobha Boba often teased me about giving her the *Khush khabri*– good news soon– a subtle nudge about having a child. Her jovial nature made her a comforting presence in my life.

We stopped at shop run by an old man whose appearance matched the ancient, crumbling walls of his shop. His toothless smile revealed sunken cheeks, and he puffed on a *Jhajri,* the smoke lazily around him, his thin, sagged neck stretching with each sip. As Shobha Boba negotiated over tobacco, I lingered by the doorway, watching the bustling street. Suddenly the air shifted. A loud crash echoed down the alley, followed by shouts that grew more urgent by the second. The crowd's energy transformed from lively to frantic, the buzz of commerce replaced by the rising crescendo of panic.

"Run!" Shoba Boba voice jolted me out of my daze. Her hand gripped my arm tightly. "Quick, we need to get home! A *danga*– riot has started!"

My heart raced as I saw people scattering in every direction. A group of soldiers appeared from one side. They carried heavy wooden sticks, striking indiscriminately at anyone within reach. My mind flashed back to soldiers who would visit our village, but these men were strangers. On the other side, local men retaliated, armed with bricks.

The street turned into a battleground. We ducked into a narrow alley, hoping to escape the chaos. The passage was so cramped that it felt like the walls were closing it on us. The crush bodies surged through the space; each person desperate to flee. My senses were overwhelmed– the heat of bodies pressing against mine, the smell of sweat and fear, the suffocating closeness. The boundaries of personal space dissolved entirely in that suffocating crush. The alley was so cramped it felt like only the absence of wedding contract separated the men and women pushing past each other.

At one point, someone's elbow jabbed my ribs, and another's hand brushed against my lower back. I couldn't tell whether it was intentional or accidental, but each touch felt invasive. The closeness was overwhelming, the kind that made you hyper-aware of every inch of your body and who was touching it.

Ahead, a vendor's cart overturned, its contents spilling into the alley, further bottlenecking the crowd. Stones flew overhead, striking walls and shattering windows. The sound of lathis meeting flesh echoed through the air, mingling with the anguish cries of those caught in the melee.

A sharp pain exploded on my forehead as a stone struck me. Blood trickled down my face, warm and sticky, but there was no time to stop. Shobha Boba's grip on my arm tightened as she pulled me forward with all her strength. When we finally reached her house, she slammed the door shut and bolted it. Both of us stood there for a moment, painting and trembling, the sounds of the riot still raging outside. The shouts and crashes seemed even louder now, reverberating off the walls of the small house.

Shobha Boba turned me and gasped. "You're bleeding!" She exclaimed; her voice thick with concern. She quickly fetched a cloth and pressed it to my forehead, her hands trembling. "You should sit," she said, guiding me to a chair. As she cleaned the wound, she murmured softly, almost to herself, "this city... it never changes. Three or four days, and everything will shut down again. That's how it always is." For her, this chaos was just another chapter in the city's story. But for me it was terrifying glimpse into a world where survival was a daily battle.

The narrow alley lingered in my mind, not just as a place but as an experience– of fear, violation and the raw instinct to survive. It was a place where boundaries blurred, where strangers became uncomfortably close, and where life was reduced to a desperate push forward.

Shobha Boba's gentle hands worked quickly, applying turmeric to the wound to stop the bleeding. "This will sting," she warned softly. I winced but said nothing. The pain felt insignificant compared to what I had just witnessed. I glanced at her face, so calm and steady despite everything. It was then that I realized how much I had to learn from her strength. Perhaps this was what Shabana Aapi had meant when she said I needed to find my freedom– not just from others but from the fear that kept me bound.

I spent the whole day indoors. The day, Shobha Boba didn't ask for any help. Instead, she insisted that I take proper rest. I went upstairs to my room, brought the same newspaper, *Ranbir,* downstairs, and began reading. As soon as Shobha Boba realized that I could still read, she was astonished. She encouraged me to continue, though the newspaper was old, and I still read it aloud to her.

It had been five days since Saleem had left for work. It was late afternoon now, and I was sitting in the kitchen with Boba, the warm sunlight streaming in through the window, casting a beam of light inside. I was absorbed in the newspaper, slowly making my way through the tiny, delicate print. The atmosphere was calm. I didn't even notice that Saleem had returned home. He stood silently at the doorway, watching us. Shobha Boba was aware of his presence, but I had no clue. As I read, my eyes shifted toward Shobha Boba, who was smiling at me. Then without warning, my gaze fell on the door. When I saw Saleem standing there, I froze. My heart skipped a beat. I quickly folded the newspaper, trying to hide my sudden unease, and turned my face away, feeling embarrassed.

As I folded the paper, I caught a glimpse of Saleem's face. For the first time, I saw him smiling. His white, shining teeth gleamed, and his neatly groomed, short beard gave him an air of composure and charm that I hadn't noticed before.

At the moment, Saleem greeted Shobha Boba and casually mentioned that the *hartal*– strike had started and would last for about three or four days. Shobha Boba then shared the details of the day, telling him about my injury. I remained facing away from them, unsure of how to behave.

Saleem entered the room and, without a word, placed his hand gently on my head, guiding me to face him. My heart raced as I felt the warmth of his touch. My eyes were cast downward, my body tensed with the anticipation of punishment. I thought he would scold me. May be even slap me for something I had done wrong. But instead of harsh words or a slap, Saleem gently grabbed my arm, helping me rise from my seat. He didn't yell or scold me– he just led me upstairs.

I hesitated, a rush of fear washing over me. I was afraid of dark, afraid that this was a punishment, that I had done something to anger him. As we entered the room, I expected him to sit down and command me to remove his shoe. But instead, he did something I didn't expect. He grabbed my arm firmly, and without saying a word, he guided me to sit on a chair. His actions were calm, but I was still confused. He placed the table aside and bent his legs gently on the floor, studying my face. His eyes moved over my wounds. Then, he reached his hand up to my forehead, pushing back the hair, I closed my eyes, bracing myself for the slap that I thought was coming. But instead, I heard him rise from the floor.

I kept my eyes shut listening, as he moved across the room. I could hear him hanging his jacket on the wall. His footsteps faded as he walked out of the room, leaving me sitting alone, still unsure of what had just happened.

I slowly rose from the chair, feeling a strange sense a relief mixed with confusion. I walked to the corner of the room, gathering the pillows around me. I sat down, my thoughts swirling. Was Saleem angry with me? Did I do something wrong? Should I have asked for permission? What if he was planning to punish me later? These thoughts spin in my mind, but my body was exhausted. The fatigue overwhelmed me, and before I knew it, sleep crept in, pulling me into a deep slumber.

A little while later, I heard the *Maghrib* call to prayer. The sound of footsteps on the stairs woke me up. Just then, Saleem knocked on the door. I opened it to find him holding a plastic bag with some fruits in one hand, and a smaller plastic bag in the other. He motioned for me to sit on the chair. I hesitated, standing still, when he said in deep voice,

"Don't you understand in one go, sit down on the chair."

I sat on the chair, and then he opened the small bag. From it, he took out a tube of medicine and began cleaning the wound on my forehead. I kept looking at his face as he worked. He opened the tube, applied it to the wound, and softly said, "it will sting, bear with it."

As he applied the medicine, he puckered his lips and blew on it. The smell of *bidi* from his mouth filled the air. This was the first time I had seen this side of him. I was stunned by his actions. Tears started flowing from my eyes, I was confused was it because of pain or his behavior? He gently wiped my tears away. May be this was what I had been missing– what I had received from Ammi, Sakina Aapi, Dayi Ammi and Subedar Dada. Maybe this was the warmth and care I needed. As my tears continued to fall, he kept wiping them away, softly and tenderly.

My eyes were drawn to his thick, naturally bordered eyebrows, which were shifting in contemplation, and his dark, black eyes. Then, from the bag, he took out a banana and an apple, placing them in front of me. In his deep voice, he said, "eat, I'll go get dinner." I was astonished. This was my responsibility, not his. Why was he doing this? It was beyond my understanding, and I found myself lost in these thoughts.

When he returned with the dinner, he placed it by the bed and gently guided me to sit on it. He put the chair beside me and sat on it himself. For the first time, we were eating together. I had only one chapati with *Nadru*– a vegetable made from lotus roots.

He ate its fill and, as usual, let out a loud burp. The only difference today was that I usually stood in front of him while he ate, but today I was sitting beside him, eating with him.

After he washed his hands, he collected the dishes and went downstairs to place them in Shobha Boba's kitchen sink. He came back quickly, telling me, "The medicine is on your forehead, remove your scarf and lie down on your back with a pillow." With a single breath, he blew at the lamp.

I began preparing myself as usual, following his command for his satisfaction. But that night, he gently lay down beside me, and I drifted off to sleep, lost in thoughts. This chaotic event had turned into something far greater for me than just an event. Undoubtedly, there was fear, a sense of terror, a new experience of life, and a deep wound that I had received. But above all, what stood out the most was Saleem's behavior– his sudden kindness, his generosity.

Eleven

I was bleeding. This was the second time in my life that the sigh of blood filled me with fear. The first time was back in the village, but Ammi was with me.

This time, Shobha Boba was by my side, but the situation was completely different. The fear felt heavier, and the pain deeper, as if the absence of Ammi's comforting presence made it all the more unbearable.

It was the era of Emergency. Indira Gandhi had imposed it. All I knew, according to Ammi, was that Hindustan was run by something called *Hakumat*– government. That word was foreign to me. I came to know about it from the newspapers. Saleem, upon seeing me reading, started bringing the *Ranbir* newspaper regularly when he was home. Often, Shobha Boba and I would sit under the sun– near the *Kiryans*– vegetable garden in the corner of the *aangan,* enclosed by a wooden fence, much like the one around the village graveyard. In that place, Boba would plant *gonglu*¸(turnip) and other vegetables, discussing the news, speculating about it. Whatever I couldn't understand, I would ask her. But every time I mentioned *hakumat,* her expression seemed to turn into that of a dried date. She was always angry at the government.

Her words carried weight. "People are happy in peace, in their trades and lives, not in conflict. But these foolish people get manipulated by politicians, becoming enemies of each other's lives." she often remarked.

One day, Saleem, Shobha Boba, and I set out towards the bazaar. Boba turned to Saleem and suggested, "let's show Noor the *Pari Mahal* today."

Saleem, who was man of few words and a personality that aligned with 'yes means yes, no means no', agreed with simple nod. We sat in a Tonga and began our journey to the Mahal. Passing through many crowded bazaars and crossing small water bridges, we finally arrived at Mahal.

As we stepped off near the entrance, Saleem pointed towards the grand structure and said, "This Mahal was built by Mughal Emperor Aurangzeb for his son." As usual, he lit his thick bidi, his signature style with one hand behind his back, and walked ahead of us.

There were various kinds of people at the Mahal. Among them was a tall, lean couple carrying bags– similar to the couple I had seen once in Kahsar Pur. One of them looked directly at me. My face was hidden under my burqa except for my eyes. He walked closer, staring intently at my eyes as if they had left mesmerized. Then he called for his wife, who had a long white hair and wore glasses. She took out a strange machine from her bag, and with gestures, signaled Saleem to stand beside me. I felt a wave of embarrassment and pulled Boba closer to me. Saleem seemed to be uncomfortable too. Then, her husband grabbed Saleem's arm and placed it on my shoulder, I could sense the discomfort in Saleem as I shivered with embarrassment.

She pointed the machine towards us and after sometime handed us a painting. It was perfect likeness of us– me, with my head reaching Saleem's shoulder, and Shobha Boba watching us. Her face, framed by hair that had turned white but was still tinged with henna red, was clear in the painting.

It was the first time I had seen myself so vividly, apart from in the mirror, and the first time I saw myself next to Saleem in this way, my head resting against his shoulder. The couple kept one painting for themselves and gave us the other.

After a while, Saleem bought us some *halwa and lawasa,* sweet pudding with salty flatbread. We began eating, I watched Boba chew. It seemed her back teeth were missing, like a mismatched rhythm in a silent performance. I couldn't help but quietly laugh to myself. We ate it and began heading back to where our Tonga was waiting. Suddenly, a loud explosion shook the air. It felt as if the ground beneath us was quaking. Chaos erupted. The smoke enveloped the area, and people began running helter-skelter, colliding into each other as they fled. Saleem signaled Boba to hurry towards the Tonga. We climbed in and started our journey home.

I turned to look back. It was scene of utter pandemonium–people stumbling, tripping, pushing each other in desperation to escape. After covering some other distance, we encountered a group of soldiers who stopped our Tonga. They ordered us to get down.

I was in my burqa. Shobha Boba instinctively moved me behind her, shielding me protectively. The soldiers commanded Saleem and the Tonga driver to lie face down on the ground with their hands on their heads. Boba and I watched in horror as they were forced down.

Then one of the soldiers approached me. He raised his stick and ordered me to remove my burqa. Boba stepped forward immediately, trying to shield me again. "She's just a child. Don't do that," she said.

They shouted at her, roughly pushing her aside. One of them grabbed my burqa and violently pulled it upwards, exposing me despite my resistance.

Shobha Boba's voice rang in my ears as the rest of the world blurred in fear and humiliation.

The soldier without any shame or decency, removed my burqa and began patting me down in the name of search. God knows what his *niyat*– intensions were, but his touch made me extremely uncomfortable. His eyes stayed fixed on mine, and there was a strange tension in his gaze. He began searching from my feet upward and was nearing my chest when another soldier, seemingly older and in charge, barked at him, "Saley! Leave the girl alone."

Reluctantly, he backed off and turned toward Shobbha Boba. They searched her too, but unlike me, she seemed somewhat familiar with such humiliations. She was muttering curses under her breath, her anger barely contained. The soldiers, seemingly done with us, then turned their attention to Saleem and Tonga driver. Meanwhile, Shobha Boba pulled me aside, wrapping in my veil, and we stood to the side, helplessly watching the scene unfold.

Without warning, the soldiers began raining blows with their batons on Saleem and the driver. They didn't stop to ask questions or understand the situation. It was blind rage and abuse of power. Unable to watch, Shobha Boba and I fell to our knees, pleading with folded hands for mercy. One soldier grabbed Saleem by ear and twisted it, shouting, "tell me! Were you involved in the blast? Do you know anything about it? Is this woman your wife?" He gestured towards me with fiery rage in his voice.

When Saleem didn't respond, the soldier sneered, "you won't speak, huh?" Just then, as Shobha Boba and I remained kneeling, pleading, one of them kicked me hard in the stomach. The force knocked me backward, and I fell to the ground. The pain was sharp and immediate, but what broke me more was Saleem's cry of anguish as he saw me collapse.

After what felt like an eternity of torture and interrogation, the soldiers let us go. We climbed back onto Tonga, beaten and shaken. Shobha Boba noticed the blood seeping through my salwar, trickling down my feet. She looked at me, her face pale with terror, her eyes wide. In a trembling voice, she shouted at Saleem, "get to the nearest hospital– quickly. She's miscarrying!"

I was in pain, but I hadn't fully realized what was happening. The fear and the chaos had numbed me. It wasn't until I saw the blood that the reality of it hit me. I felt like a lifeless shell, and before I could process anything everything went dark.

When I opened my eyes, the first thing I saw was a white ceiling. The smell of medicine filled the air. I glanced around and saw Saleem sitting at the edge of my bed, his face buried in his hands, lost in thought. On the other side, Shobha Boba was holding my hand tightly.

As soon as she noticed I was awake, her face lit up with relief. It was the kind of joy I had seen on her face only once before– when her son Aditya had visited her after a long time. But even then, that joy was fleeting. She never let Aditya stay with her for more than a day, fearing someone might kill him, just like her husband.

Shobha Boba squeezed my hand gently and said, "Noor, don't worry. You're still young. Life will give you more chances."

Her words were a reminder of the *khushkhabri,* the good news, she always teased me about, the one she had been so excited for. But now that seemed like a distant, bitter memory.

As I lay there, consciousness slowly returning, flashes of my village came back to me. Memories of how Ammi had lost a life in similar way. I couldn't stop questioning myself– why was history repeating itself? Ammi used to say *muqadar*– destiny is unique to everyone, but was it?

I turned to look at Saleem. His face was grim and hopeless. He didn't say a word– just placed his hand softly on my head and walked out of the room. His silence left me with endless questions. Was he disappointed with the situation? Was he grieving the loss of what could've been? Or was he heartbroken at seeing me in pain?

Some questions, I realized, remain unanswered, locked within us. Perhaps that was foundation of our relationship too– a union defined by silence. We were together yet our conversations were only functional. Saleem's quiet nature contrasted sharply with the storm of thoughts in my mind, a storm of books and the words I desperately wanted to share.

But instead of sharing, I found myself talking to the walls of our room. They were my audience– the left was my Dayi Ammi, right was Ammi, near the bed was Sakina Aapi and by the door was Saleem, listening to every thought, every line I spoke aloud. And sometimes those same words would echo back, overwhelming my heart and mind, consuming me entirely.

Now, I had to live with the bitter reality, just I always had. When a person's mind and thoughts empower them, the person becomes nothing more than a living corpse.

Twelve

In Kahsar Pur, *Harud* was a celebration of innocence. Tahir and I would gather golden leaves into towering heaps, only to dive into them with carefree laughter. The crisp air would carry the earthy scent of fallen leaves, mingling with the faint aroma of wood smoke from distant *Chulas*. It was a season of joy for me and Tahir as well, a time when the village seemed smaller and warmer, wrapped in golden embrace of nature, but for some, it wasn't. Everyone carries their own stories, their own burdens.

I remember a *Harud,* when I was in the fields with Ammi. The ground was littered with dry leaves, and I was joyfully gathering them into little piles to play with. Ammi, however, seemed distant, lost in her thoughts.

That was the season Baba had called her *manhoos*– a word I overheard when I wasn't meant to. Perhaps Ammi had lost a small life, one she had buried in the graveyard and in her soul.

"Ammi are you upset with Baba for calling you *manhoos*?" I asked her with a child's innocence, expecting anger, tears, or perhaps silence.

Instead, Ammi responded in soft, weary voice, on that seemed to carry years of pain.

"No, Noor, I'm not upset," she said, her gaze fixed on the horizon. "I'm just shedding some memories that sit heavy on my soul, like a weight I can no longer bear."

Her words confused me then, but the metaphor lingered in my mind. She pointed to the trees, their branches stripped bare by the season.

"Do you see these trees? They shed their leaves so that new ones can grow in their place– leaves that will bring new life, a new year, new hope and a fresh harvest. People should learn from trees, Noor. We need to let go bad memories, the pain and the burdens we carry. Only then can we move forward and truly witness the spring in our lives."

I didn't fully understand her then, but the truth of her words echoed in the crisp autumn air. I watched her as she sat, quiet and resolute, letting go of the weight she carried. It wasn't just a season for the trees– it was a season for her as well.

But today, in this unfamiliar city, the scene was different. I stood at a distance, watching the same golden leaves scatter across the ground, untouched and unclaimed. There was no Tahir, no laughter, no childish games. The leaves were not a part of my joy anymore– they were a reminder of what I had left behind.

Here, *Harud* felt foreign, almost aloof. The leaves dance in the wind, but their beauty didn't reach me the same way. I realized that sometimes, it is not the season that changes, but the eyes with which we see it. The golden leaves were the same, but today I was merely an observer– detached, longing and somewhere deep inside, a little lost.

This autumn had painted the ground golden with fallen leaves, turning the earth into an untouched canvas. Amid this natural artwork, humans, animals and birds went about their business, as if oblivious to the beauty under their feet. The sharp, melancholic chirp of *Kane-Kaw,* Himalayan bulbul echoed in the crisp air, announcing the arrival of autumn.

I was in the kitchen with Shobha Boba, helping her prepare breakfast. The warmth of the tandoor filled the room as she skillfully placed raw dough on its hot walls, and I, with my clumsy hands, handed her flattened bread that landed with a resounding slap.

Just then, Saleem entered from the courtyard, coughing– a deliberate sound, almost like a doorbell, to alert those inside of his arrival. He stepped in and, without any preamble, said to Shobha Boba, "Shobha Poph! – he used to call her Poph, paternal aunt. I need to go to Mandi Nagar for work. It might take fifteen-sixteen days. I think I'll take Noor along."

Shobha Boba, ever composed, smiled and replied, "sure, take her. She's yours, after all." Then, with her usual nonchalance, she took a puff from the burning *jhajri*, exhaling the smoke playfully in my direction. Saleem gave a slight nod and went upstairs to pack, while I stood there, stunned. We had spent the entire night together, and yet he hadn't mentioned this to me.

I hurriedly packed my bag, and Shobha Boba, with her nurturing touch, tucked a small, transparent bottle of her homemade garlic pickle into my bag. "Take this," she said, before whispering her signature farewell– *khushkhabri* into my ear. As she stood by the doorframe, her hands resting on its edges, she watched us until we disappeared into the narrow alley.

It was my first bus journey, from our bustling local market to Mandi Nagar, where Saleem worked. Before this, I had never sat on a bus. I only used to sit on the Tongas.

The bus was a sight to behold– faded green paint, chipped away to reveal rusty metal underneath, and seats so narrow that they barely fit one person, let alone two. The roof was laden with luggage, from sacks of rice to pots and pans, held together precariously by fraying ropes. The interior smelled of damp wool, sweat and the faint odor of tobacco– Saleem's bidi included.

The bus was already overflowing with passengers when we arrived, a chaotic mix of men, women and children, each clutching into their belongings as if they were extensions of their bodies. A wiry man with a shrill voice, shouted the names of destinations in quick successions, urging passengers to board or alight.

As the bus jolted forward, I found myself standing amidst the crowd, pressed uncomfortably close to strangers. Men and women bumped into one another with each sharp turn or sudden break. Saleem, bound by his introverted nature and a deep-seated hesitation to express emotions openly, didn't make any effort to shield me from the jostling crowd. Perhaps it wasn't just Saleem– all the men seemed preoccupied with their own struggles, failing to protect their wives from the chaos around them.

After what felt like an eternity of standing, the wiry man–conductor finally directed us to vacant seats. But instead of sitting together, I ended up next to a stranger, and Saleem was seated elsewhere. As I sat there, the thought crossed my mind: Couldn't Saleem have asked for an exchange, just once? Or is this some unspoken rule of bus travel.

The conductor's voice punctuated my thoughts, showing the names of upcoming stops. At every halt, the bus groaned under the weight of new passengers, while others disembarked. I watched Saleem from my seat. He sat with his unusual calm demeanor, one hand on the seat and other holding his bidi, staring out the window as if lost in thought.

My own soulmate, a middle-aged woman with a bundle of *kunzalwan* in her lap, offered me a sympathetic smile. Her presence was comforting, though we didn't exchange a word. I glanced back at Saleem, wondering if he even cared about this physical distance between us, or if he simply accepted it as a part of journey.

The bus ride was more than just a physical journey– it was reflecting of the silent, restrained dynamics of my relationship with Saleem. His silence, his inability to express care in ways I hoped for, left me questioning: was this just his nature, or was it deeper taboo woven into the fabric of our lives?

As the bus rumbled on, the sun dipped lower, casting long shadows over the winding roads. The chaos inside began to settle, but the question in my heart stirred restlessly, demanding answers Saleem might never give.

As soon as we stepped off the bus, Saleem guided me for a short walk. He didn't say a word, just led me to a quiet spot where he placed the bags down. Without even glance in my direction, he turned and walked away. The evening was settling in, and the coolness of the air reminded me that I hadn't prayed yet. The streets were unfamiliar, filled with strangers. Some looked at me with a fleeting sympathy, others with eyes that seemed to bore into me– judging, calculating– without a word. The silence was suffocating.

After sometime, Saleem returned, flanked by two men who seemed to tower him. Their bellies hung out like swollen bags, their bodies swaying with every step. They looked exactly like the men Ammi used to draw for me when teaching me to write on slate, exaggerated figures she used to describe as– Saith (merchant)

One of them– short, with a rough stubble and a grin that didn't reach his eyes– looked me up and down, his gaze lingering longer than it should have. Then turning to Saleem, he spoke in a voice thick with mockery, "what's this, brother? Brought yourself a little treat for yourself? Where did you find her? She looks young– fresh. Get one for us too? Or should we take her off your hands?" his laugh was sharp, cruel, like the crack of a whip.

The other man, a bit older, slapped Saleem on the back so hard it echoed in the quiet street. "Brother, you're hiding her well! You have something good with you! Don't worry, we won't take her, not today," he added, his voice laced with mock friendliness.

I stood there, frozen, my heart pounding in my chest, listening to the venom drip from their words. The whole world seemed to collapse into that moment– one of those rare instances when silence screams louder than my words ever could. My body felt numb. I was on the edge of something dark and deep, but I couldn't move, couldn't speak.

I turned to look Saleem, waiting for him to say something– anything. His face remained expressionless, like a mask made of stone. His silence was heavy, suffocating. He just chuckled, the sound hollow and empty, before turning away from men. They walked off, still laughing, but Saleem didn't flinch. He didn't defend me. He didn't say a word.

The men disappeared into the crowd, their laughter fading into the distance. Saleem picked up the bags, his hands moving mechanically. Without a glance at me, my mind in turmoil, my heart sinking deeper with each step.

Why did he stay silent? The question spun around and around in my mind. He reminded me of Tahir, how Tahir had defended me in front of Afzal, how he suffered, and how urged me to escape from there. A deep, cold realization hit me, sharp and brutal: Maybe just maybe, I shouldn't have left Tahir alone that day. The guilt gnawed at me, harder and I walked behind Saleem.

Finally, we reached a narrow street, crowded and chaotic, with a lone house at the end. It stood like a forgotten thing, with a low, crooked root that looked like it had been put together with no more than hope and rust. Saleem unlocked the door, motioning for me to step inside.

I paused for moment, my heart heavy in my chest, before stepping into the darkness that awaited me. The door shut behind me with a soft click, and in that instant, the world outside seemed to vanish, leaving only the oppressive weight of silence and the unknown.

The room reeked of raw, damp earth– a smell that clung to the air like a ghost of its past. Scattered across the floor, bits and pieces of life lay abandoned: crumpled papers, broken glass, and the odd trinkets of a forgotten existence. In the far corner, a cracked wooden trunk sat as though burdened with the weight of untold stories. Its lid was slightly ajar, and peeking out from it was the leg

of a woman's salwar, faded and limp, as if had witnessed far too much. That single fragment of cloth held my attention longer than I anticipated, whispering silent tales of someone who had one lived, breathed, and perhaps even suffered within these very walls.

A dim, yellow bulb hung from the ceiling, its glass mottled with grime and time. Its weak glow barely illuminated the room, casting shadows that seemed to move of their own accord. This place was supposed to be in the city, yet it felt light-years away from the simplicity of village life– not in advancement, but in the sheer absence of soul. Saleem left shortly after unlocking the door, returning later with a modest meal for dinner.

While he was gone, I busied myself with cleaning, trying to make sense of the chaos that surrounded me. Behind the door, I found a garbage bin, overflowing with scraps and remnants of stories no one cared to keep. The refuse told its own version of truth– secrets buried deep within these four walls, voices stifled before they could be heard, memories discarded like trash. I couldn't help out but wonder: how many untold lives were erased here.?

After dinner, we lay down on the cold, unforgiving floor, the silence between us heavier than the air itself. Saleem, as if out of habit, placed his hand on my shoulder– a familiar gesture I'd come to expect but never embrace. It was his signal, his quiet demand, a wordless expectation that I would comply. Tonight, though, something was different. My lips didn't refuse him, but my body did. It stiffened, recoiled, as though an invisible wall had risen between us.

I stared at the cracked ceiling, replaying the day's events in my mind. Why had he stayed silent? Their words still echoed in my ears– mocking, cruel. And his silence? It was deafening, as if he'd handed me over their judgement without a fight. That moment lingered, gnawed at me like a wound that refused to heal.

Is this what a relationship is? I wondered. Built in the darkness, nurtured behind the closed doors, only to be hidden from the world? A relationship forged in secrecy, hidden within four walls, is no different from the kind that flourishes in the shadow of grand palaces– or the sordid confines of brothels.

I thought of relationships society deems respectable– the ones displayed proudly in public, without shame or hesitation, just like the couple I saw in Kahsar Pur. A bond that requires no validation, no justification, just like Ammi and Dayi, Ammi and Sakina Aapi. If relationship born out of purity, one sanctioned by faith, still feels like a taboo to share with the world, then what truly separates it from illicit.?

I questioned the *bunyaad* of what we had. If he couldn't defend me before others, couldn't claim me his own without hesitation, then what was this? Was this relationship any different from those formed in moments of fleeting lust, behind curtains of shame and denial? And those women– the ones men hide in the shadows of their youth, only to pride in their old age as forgotten mistresses– was their foundation ever truly built to last?

The room seemed to grow darker, colder, as these thoughts wrapped themselves around me like a shroud. This was another unsolved mystery in a life already riddled with unanswered questions. Eventually, exhaustion took over, and I slipped into a restless sleep, the silence of the room echoing louder than any words ever could.

The very next day, I woke up to the noise of the bustling market outside. People were moving towards their daily business, and the air was alive with the sounds of chatter and commotion. Saleem was already awake, sitting by the corner of the room. He was dressed in fresh clothes, ready to step out. Perhaps he had been waiting for me to wake up and lock the door from the inside.

I felt a tinge of guilt from the night before. As I got up, Saleem looked at me, his voice almost pleading,

“Noor, come with me. I’ll show you the place where I work.” I didn’t want to go, but as I glanced around the room, the suffocating walls and stale air seemed unbearable. I thought, maybe it was better to step out, to feel the open air on my face. Reluctantly, I agreed.

We locked the door and stepped out onto the street. The market was alive with the vibrant chaos– buses honking, small carts rolling by, and even horse-drawn carriages adding to the melody of the scene. Every face we passed seemed to carry his own story, or maybe it was just my mind searching for tales in the depths of every passing expression. As we moved, the street grew narrower, and the bustling crowd seemed to press closer.

Suddenly, Saleem grabbed my arm to help me cross the road. For the first time, he held my hand in public. I couldn’t help but stare at him. His side profile was sharp, his face slightly aged but still gentle. A single white strand in his beard caught my attention, floating near his lips as he spoke. My focus stayed on him even as he guided me through the chaos. My mind, however, was still replaying last night, and the guilt heavy.

Even after crossing the road, Saleem didn't let go of my hand. I was surprised but didn't protest. A little further, we came across an old wooden bridge. Saleem stopped in the middle and pointed down at the river with his *shahadat* finger "Look," he said softly.

The river flawed beneath us, sometimes raging with white foam, other times eerily still. It reminded of my own life– turbulent in some moments, stagnant in others. I got lost in the scene, staring at the water as if it carried the answers to all my unspoken questions. Saleem gently waved his hand in front of my eyes, pulling me out of my thoughts.

We walked on, and today, for some reason, Saleem didn't light his usual bidi. Instead, he held my hand firmly, as though afraid to let go. It felt strange but comforting.

The marketplace opened up ahead, and the first thing I noticed was an old, worn clock tower standing tall amidst the crowd. Beneath its booksellers sat on the ground, surrounded by stacks of old and new books. Shouting out the prices and titles to passersby. Saleem guided me towards them, showing me a few books as if he was trying to share a piece of his world. He bought a small notebook and led me into the crowd.

Eventually, we arrived at his workplace, a large open ground filled with tongas, carts, and few small trucks. It was bustling with activity– men loading goods onto carts and shouting instructions. Saleem gestured for me to sit on a bench at the corner and wait. He walked toward the shed where the loading was taking place. He opened the same notebook, sat on the chair and began writing something. At the same time, he started assigning tasks to the other workers, ensuring everyone was engaged in their duties.

I sat quietly, observing the scene. My gaze wandered to the bustling market corner, where vegetable and fruit vendors had spread out sacks on the ground, showing a variety of produce. Amidst the greens, my eyes caught the sigh of familiar *dheed,* fern and other vegetables that Sakina Aapi often dried on sacks outside her house. A thought struck me– perhaps Tahir came here to sell vegetables. This fleeting memory turned the village and Tahir into a beautiful fragment of my past as my eyes instinctively searched for him in the crowd. As my eyes searched restlessly, a scene suddenly pulled me in, breaking my trance and drawing my focus entirely.

A woman was dragging a man by the collar, shouting at him with a rage that needed no words to be understood. Her furious gestures and sharp eyes told a story of their own. The scene triggered a memory– Hashim Chacha and Shamshada Chachi from my village. I recall how we would see them fighting almost every week, Hashim Chacha always overpowering her, leaving Shamshada Chachi with bruises and tears.

Ammi's voice echoed in my mind; her lessons etched deep within me. She would always say, "Noor, every human is born with equal rights. If you fail to honor those rights in your relationships or work, the world will disgrace you, and so will the afterlife."

Whenever I saw something frightening in the village, the most terrifying for me was the beating– etched into my memory from witnessing it with Ammi. As a child, whenever such moments unfolded, if Ammi stood, I would hide under kameez; if she sat, I'd bury myself beneath the shawl. But now seeing the same scene before me, fear clawed at my chest differently. It wasn't just the present but haunting memories of Baba, Afzal and night soldiers. I could feel the same childhood dread, the primal need for my mother's protection, the warmth of safety she used to shield me with.

But here those lessons felt blurred. Both the woman and the man seemed honest in their anger. Yet something was fundamentally wrong. Was it their honesty or was it the *bunyaad* of their relationship that was flawed?

I sat there, lost in thought, the crowd moving around me like a tide. Saleem was somewhere in the tide, and so was I, caught between memories, guilt, and the unspoken truths of life.

Thirteen

The scorching summer sun made the air dense as the villagers gathered to cut grass. It was a traditional, a ritual, repeated every week on alternate days. Men, women and children worked together in the fields. Ammi kept me at Dayi's house, taking care of the cut pumpkins that were left to dry for winter.

Parveen as usual stayed at home under special care of Baba, I always saw her belly big and round, like it was full of something. Ammi always warned me to stay away from her. Parveen was very close to her younger brother Nadir– who had monkey-like hair, golden beard and reddish face. Every time Nadir visited Parveen's house something troublesome would happen, which is why the villagers would call him "Nadir Badmash" – the trouble maker. He was an avid hashish smoker and good friend with Afzal. Ammi would always warn me saying, "They both are same in their actions, stay away from them."

These two would often sit by the path near the spring water, teasing the girls and women of the village as they passed by. Some women who criticized them were likely frustrated with them, while others especially young girls who didn't criticize them seemed to enjoy their actions. Parveen, on the other hand, would use Nadir to humiliate Ammi and me. Since Baba never said anything to Nadir, he often called me "*lawaris*" –unwanted.

That day I was standing in the *aangan* of Dayi Ammi's house, looking at the scene, I saw the men working on one side and the women on the other, all busy cutting the grass together. The sigh was like a procession of colorful ants working in unison. Each moving with purpose. The energy in the air was vibrant, almost as if everything in the world has paused to watch this spectacle. It felt surreal, almost like an exaggeration of life itself, with people working tirelessly under the blistering sun. They were singing some songs loudly and one person playing Raft, the sound gradually reaching my ears in intervals, carried by the soft breeze. Perhaps it was this very melody that kept them working tirelessly together as one, or maybe it was the feast being prepared at Shabana Baji's house, the aroma of which occasionally drift towards me with breeze.

Then, Tahir appeared before me, grinning as usual, the oil from the hair on the left side dripping down on the left side dripping down onto his eyes, wearing brownish Salwar Kameez. He reached into his neatly tucked pockets and pulled out some hashish balls. This was our currency, the reason we could get, *dhingri, gachak* and other things. He said to me, with his lisping voice,

"Nool, let's go quickly to the shop, then we will visit Shabana Baji's house."

Tahir had this habit of throwing stones while walking, not with the intent of hitting someone, but just to see it could hit a target.

"Look, Nool, I'm going to hit that tree," he would say, throwing atones at it. Sometimes he would succeed, sometimes not. When he missed, he'd laugh and say, "Where I aimed, I had already thought of it in my heart." Even when he failed, he would laugh it off and say, "Do you believe me now, Nool? I'm a dangerous marksman. I once hit a leopard from far away." I knew this was a tall tale, but his blunders were always so entertaining, especially with his lisp. I would smile, nod, and close my eyes in a small gesture of agreement. I had to agree after all, because Tahir was the one who was no less than a treasure for me.

We quickly made our way down the path, as usual, Tahir was hitting targets with his stones. We reached at Subedar Dada's shop, where he exchanged the hashish balls secretly and bought my sweets and a *gulail,* slingshot. This was probably the first time we had bought something to play beside sweets. He started boasting "Now, I'll be using this to hit targets."

As we ate sweets and made our way back, we saw two people on the curve of our village path, the place where the villagers usually rested.

"Who are these people?" I asked Tahir. He just laughed and said, "Let it be, I'll hit them with *gulail,"* as if he had just achieved a monumental feat. When we reached the top, we saw Nadir and Parveen. They called us over. Parveen shouted at me, "You! *Lawaris,* stand here you two-eyed bitch!"

Tahir, the scoundrel, was also called over. Parveen accused us of injuring her sheep with stones. She ordered Nadir to teach us lesson, especially me.

"Take care of these two *haramis* and show them a good lesson," She shouted before going towards the house.

Nadir, sitting with his legs crossed, was smoking. He looked at us with half-closed eyes and said, "Follow me." We were terrified and had no choice but to follow him as he led us toward a desolate area, far from the village. There he made us sit, as if we were criminals awaiting punishment. At that moment, Shahida arrived– the most notorious girl in the village. There were rumors that something was going on between her and Nadir. She was out in the fields cutting grass and ended up joining Nadir.

Shahida shared a good bond with both me and Ammi. Ammi had given her two suits, one green and one maroon, which no longer fit Ammi. Shahida would often visit us and was always kind and affectionate towards me. When I saw her there, I felt a wave of relief wash over me. But the scenario was different. Nadir shouted at Tahir and me, ordering, "Come here, empty your pockets, and place everything in front."

Terrified, we did as he said. Then Nadir started teasing both of us. He taunted Tahir saying, "Say it once– Rasheed is your father!" and burst out laughing.

Turning to me, he sneered, "You're a stray– your mother doesn't even know." Both of them laughed loudly. I didn't expect this from Shahida, especially since Ammi also trusted her.

Then Nadir said, "Turn the other way, raise your hands, and stand still." He pushed our kameez into our backsides with his hands and said,

"Whosever's kameez's comes out first will get slaps on their back." Both of them began laughing, enjoying the humiliation they were causing us.

After scolding us for a while, Nadir leaned over and whispered something in Shahida's ear, resting his arm on her shoulder. Then he turned towards us and said,

"Alright, illegitimate son, you can go. I'll let her leave in a bit." Without thinking, Tahir quickly refused, "Let her go. I'll bring you more hashish balls, and you can take my *gulail.*" Nadir agreed, and we were let go. Tahir sacrificed his slingshot, and we ran towards the village, our feet kicking up powdery dust.

As we ran, I couldn't but wonder, was Tahir more sensible than me, or was it because of me that he found himself in these situations. Ammi's words echoed in my mind: "Some people are blessed by God, but they realize their value when they are gone."

Today, just like the dust of village paths, I was running through the city streets, but the difference wat that here, the rainwater was soaking my salwar. The city streets were narrow, and the smell of the wet mud clung to my clothes, every step of mine making noise. The loneliness of the city, the fear of the unknown, closed in around me. That day, although my steps were small in the village, but the *manzil,* destination was clear. But today, my steps, though more confident, were uncertain as I rushed towards Saleem's workplace.

I remembered Ammi's words again:

"The *Shaitaan* lies in the heart, Noor, and sometimes it wears the mask of love."

Today, Gausi, someone I had recently considered a friend, had revealed that mask for what it truly was.

Fourteen

Gausi, a woman I met here in Mandi Nagar. One day, Saleem had gone to work and I was sitting alone outside the room, leaning against the doorframe, soaking in the soft morning sun. from the narrow lane in front of me, I saw a robust woman whose every part of her body swayed rhythmically with her graceful, sashaying walk, someone who looked as perfect as the image of a beautiful lady holding a beauty cream on the last page of Ranbir newspaper, the very paper I had read cover to cover three times. She came closer and asked me,

"Are you new here?" I nodded in affirmation.

Then, without hesitation, she sat beside me and started conversation as if she had been looking for me all along. Strangely enough, I felt comfortable too. I thought, it's better to chat a little rather than talk to the walls all day. That day, we sat together until the time for *Zohar* prayers.

She was extremely talkative, almost like Shobha Aapi's ducks, going quack, quack, quack, without ever stopping. Gausi narrated stories about how she went to school, how many male friends she had made, and how her love affair had failed twice–

once because she ditched the guy for not being handsome enough, and the second time because the man was already married. For me these stories sounded like sinful confessions, yet I strangely enjoyed talking to her. As we exchanged laughter, she playfully slapped my shoulder and laughed loudly, revealing a decayed tooth in the process.

I don't know why, I felt a sense of belonging with her. Her way of talking compelled me to consider her a friend. Saleem was usually at work– leaving early in the morning and often returning late at night, sometimes even after midnight, and occasionally not until the next day.

We had initially come here for fifteen days, but it had already been over a month. Whenever I asked Saleem about returning, he would reassure me, saying, "Just a few more days, and then we will go back and start building our home near Shobha Poph's place."

During the day, I spent most of my time chatting with Gausi. She entertained me with gossip from her neighborhood, indulging in endless stories and backbiting. Every day, she would come with new stories and tales. I often wondered how different our lives were. I had no such tales to laugh about– or maybe I had too but didn't want to dig them up. Gausi came every day with fresh gossip and rumors, and in no time, she had told me about every household in the lane. She knew whose husband was whose, who was having an affair, and where someone's wife secretly went. She even narrated how one lady left her husband and seven children to run away and marry a boy half her age.

I still remember one particular story she told me that had me laughing so hard my lower six ribs started hurting. She shared that a lady in her neighborhood had nine children, born like steps on a staircase. She added with a cheeky grin, "Thank God her husband got afflicted with piles; it's been two years now, and the situation has finally come to a halt."

A few days later, she came strutting towards me, glowing with her usual flair, and said, "Get ready, O queen of the four walls! Come, I'll show you the world."

I couldn't resist. Not even once did I think about what Saleem would say, because by now, the bond of trust between me and Gausi had grown incredibly strong. I quickly changed my clothes, threw on my burqa, and was ready.

She glanced at me and said, "Don't wear that burqa." When I refused, she insisted and instead offered a suggestion:

"Just cover your face. Let your body feel the air a little." Reluctantly, I agreed to compromise. I covered my face and head with black shawl, leaving only my eyes visible.

Gausi looked at me and dramatically exclaimed,

"Your two colorful, killer eyes! Today, the city is going to witness a massacre."

We locked the door and set out. She led me through every alley and corner of the city. In the crowded bazaar, she walked with her usual sway, winking flirtatiously at passing men. Today, I noticed something significant– whether you're in a burqa or not, people will stare at you.

We sat at sweet shop, where she joked and chatted with the *halwai*, quickly getting frank with him. Then, we wandered into a park where couples sat scattered around, some in secluded corners, others in plain sight, sharing their stories with one another.

Some women were veiled, some were not. As we walked past the couples, Gausi made a point of swaying even more dramatically in front of them. She turned to me, whispering,

"Watch this. Her partner will stare at me, and they'll end up fighting."

And sure enough, I counted at least three or four pairs whose arguments she managed to spark. After spending the entire day wandering around, we finally headed home.

This routine continued, and I often wondered, how does she stay happy and maintain such a childlike spirit? Even though she was much older than me.

She loved teasing people, pulling their legs, and stirring up arguments– it all seemed to entertain her. Every day, she would write "Ritu" with coal on the walls outside Kishor's house. Yes, the same Kishore having an extra marital affair with Ritu. And every day, she gave Kishore extra work by making him erase the name.

After Tahir, she was the one with whom I laughed freely, uninhibitedly. True, some of her habits didn't align with my ideals, but perhaps they were perfect for her own world. It started to dawn on me that society shapes a person's character, forcing them to wear a façade that eventually becomes their reality.

Gausi never shared much about her past. She only spoke of her affairs, leaving her childhood veiled in secrecy. Some truths are too deep, some voices forever silenced, creating a world within a world– nonexistent, yet potent. Perhaps that's why we see some people lost in their own reality, wandering on streets, and dismiss them as mad. Perspectives shape worlds, just as they shape people. Some find rest in sleep, while others collapse from exhaustion, calling it peace.

Gausi, like a coin, had two sides. Today she was finally ready to reveal the mystery of the salwar which was hanging in the old wooden box when we first entered in this room. It caught Gausi's attention while she was helping me with cleaning. She immediately picked up the salwar and said, "This was here? I've been searching for it at home for so long!"

I didn't quite understand and asked, "What do you mean?"

She picked up the salwar and said, "There's a deep secret behind this; someday, I'll tell you what it is."

That evening, just before sunset, there were fine, tiny raindrops falling, but at times, they weren't enough to soak the clothes. Gausi and I went to her house. It was my first time visiting. I had often asked her before,

"Gausi, take me to your home sometime," but she would always snap back,

"What will you do there? There's nothing to see."

After crossing three narrow lanes, we finally arrived at her house. The gate, made of rusted iron, creaked loudly as it opened. Inside was a large *aangan*, with two old rooms standing opposite each other. The grime on the door handles of those rooms hinted at how ancient they were, each handle a testament to years of neglect.

In the *aangan,* lying on a cot, was Gausi's father. He was shirtless, frail and paralyzed on one side. His head and hand were twisted unnaturally to one side, as if permanently frozen in that position. The moment I saw him; I couldn't help but feel a sudden urge to laugh. His appearance struck me as odd, almost comical, but I quickly suppressed the laughter building inside me.

Every few moments, her father would try to mumble something, his paralyzed tongue slurring the words into incomprehensible fragments. Only the sound "Gaaa..." was clear, the rest of his words drowning in a jumble of noised. I realized he was trying to call out ton Gausi.

After a while, Gausi turned to me and said,

"Let's go, Noor. I can't breathe here anymore." There was heaviness in her tone, something I had never heard before.

As we walked out of the *aangan,* Gausi finally broke her silence. Behind her playful face and mischievous eyes lay secrets that were too heavy for her young shoulders. She revealed one of them to me that day.

"Noor, she began, her voice flat and emotionless.

"My mother left us. She ran with a traveler and never came back. I hate her. How can a mother abandon her four-year-old daughter? She abandoned me and my father like we were nothing. Because of that mother, I still suffer to this day. Forget it; you won't understand."

I looked at Gausi's face– her cheeks were red, and tears were streaming down her face.

I stayed silent, unsure what to say. It was a truth that explained so much– the rusted doors, the lonely *aangan,* the lifeless gaze of her father. Gausi carried it all, this broken home and the scars it left behind.

That evening Gausi asked me to wear red salwar suit. As we left her house, walking through the bazaar, we stopped to relish the colorful ice gola sold by famous Rustum kaka, whose words were as sweet as honey, according to Gausi he was a *muqbir–*

whistleblower. Watching him scrape ice off a large block, I couldn't help but wonder about its origin.

"This is factory-made," Gausi explained.

It reminded me of my village, where we stored food and milk in the tiny underground rooms called– *Doud Daer,* near the local spiring, keeping them fresh. Lost in thoughts, we drifted from the bustling market to a quieter street.

"Where are you taking me?" I asked, half intrigued, half apprehensive.

"Relax," she smirked, "Today, I'll show you the secret behind the four walls– the helplessness of some and enjoyment of others– under the dark veil of the night. And of course, as promised, the secret behind the salwar."

We humans are strange beings; we love delving into the secrets of other's lives. Sometimes, the curiosity to discover makes a person great– like I read in the newspaper about how Hindustan became nuclear country. I have no idea what that means, but I understood that it became powerful. Telephones, too, are an invention born out of curiosity. Some poor soul must have grown tired of whistling and shouting, so they invented the telephone.

After a while, we reached a neighborhood with elegant houses. Sitting at the corner of the lane, Gausi asked me to wait. Soon, a frail man approached us. He was so thin; it seemed his face was merely a canvas for two large eyes. His barren expression mirrored a life of deprivation. He led us to a lavish house with gleaming white marble floors. Inside, we settled onto plush sofas.

Moments later, a portly man with a disproportionately large belly entered. He gestured something to Gausi, and she left with him, asking me to wait. When she returned, her hair was disheveled, and her face unreadable. A knot of unease tightened in my chest. Before I could question her, a tall-man in tourist like attire walked in, his piercing gaze tracing me from feet to head. Panicked, I curled my toes and gripped the sofa.

He moved toward me, “Who’s this new delightful thing whose cheeks and body alluring?”

Was my body like this? This was the first time any man had said this to me, but even he said it in a cold tone.

“A friend,” Gausi replied, her tone flat.

The man’s gaze shifted to me; his eyes lingering. “Friend, huh? Doesn’t look like she belongs here.”

I felt a shiver run down my spine. "Gausi, what is this place?" I asked, my voice barely above whisper.

"Relax," she said, but her eyes didn't meet mine.

The man stepped closer, his eyes scanning me like I was prey. "She's pretty," he remarked, reaching out to touch my arm, I yanked it free and bolted toward the gate. My feet carried me through the same streets, barefoot, not daring to look back. I found myself outside, gasping for air, my heart pounding. It was the same path we had walked, but now it felt like an escape from an abyss.

Without stopping, I ran, away from the darkness that had engulfed me, away from the streets I wished I had never uncovered.

I ran all the way to Saleem's workplace without looking back. Saleem saw me and, panic-stricken, rushed towards me. He embraced me tightly.

Was it real? Yes, it was. Perhaps some incidents change people forever.

Ammi used to say, Noor, every step of life will teach you something." In reality, recognizing faces and true intensions was the hardest thing.

Today Gausi felt like a betrayer– not because she bought me to strange place, but because I finally understood the truth behind the salwar hanging outside the wooden box.

Some betrayals aren't born of malice– they're born of circumstances we can't see. In Gausi's story, I saw cracks in society's foundation, the hidden pain behind her laughter. Life isn't about judging others for their choices; it's about understanding the battles they fight. Sometimes, the people we trust the most teach us the most painful yet profound lessons.

Fifteen

Some words have a strange existence, a truth I only realized today. One such word is *"Laanch,"* transgender. A word I saw brought to life, dancing at a wedding.

I had often heard boys in Kahsar Pur hurl this word at each other, using it as a weapon to insult and belittle. I remember an incident when Shakeel had struck Yahya on the head with a stone, leaving a deep gash. It was not because Yahya had taken the fish caught by him from the river. All because Yahya had called Shakeel *"Laanch".* This matter reached home, and a fight broke out between the two households. The fight escalated so much that the village council meeting had to be called.

Sanaullah Chobdar, the oldest man in the village– or at least he looked like it– was tasked with resolving such disputes. Now, calling him a figure of authority would be a stretch. With a bright red henna-dyed beard and his signature walking stick that served more as a prop for his failing legs than a symbol of power, Chobdar was both amusing and, frankly embarrassing.

At first glance, he appeared as a man who had weathered life's storms, but a closer look revealed something much more comical.

His loose skin hung like curtains over his wiry frame, his lips were perpetually smacking together as if savoring some imaginary feast, and his few remaining teeth jutted out in awkward angles. Yet, despite this caricature of old age, Chobdar's eyes betrayed his greatest flaw– they were as restless and naughty as boy spying through the cracks of a fence.

According to Ammi no woman was spared the scan of those stargazing eyes. Be she village elder or a newlywed bride, Chobdar's eyes followed her like a moth to a flame. His obsession was no secret, and the villagers laughed behind his back. But the humor turned into frustration when his third youngest wife, Rehana, came into the picture. Rehana was a beautiful, spirited woman half his age, and gossip swirled that she had no patience for her aging husband. Even at the council meetings, when Chobdar was supposed to be solving disputes, he could barely keep his attention on the matter at hand. The moment a woman crossed his field of vision; his neck would snap in her direction so quickly that his sycophants often joked, "Chobdar needs a glass of milk again."

That day, Shobha Boba rummaged through her ancient wooden trunk. With a triumphant smile, she pulled out a heavy, vibrant red suit, its hue as bold as the bindi on her forehead. she handed it to me and said, wear this *Taranga.* It was a traditional dress, embroidered and intricate.

"We are going to Nitya's wedding," she added.

Nitya was Boba's brother's only daughter, the eldest among her siblings, with three younger brothers waiting in line.

I held the dress in my hands, its weigh reminding me of the expectations that came with it.

Attending this wedding had two purposes. First, as Boba excitedly declared, "*Laanch* is coming to dance and sing!"

Second, I wanted to witness a wedding filled with grand preparations and excitement unlike the simple ceremonies in my village.

We set off for the wedding. By this time, Saleem had shifted his business here in Jeevapur after an incident we only knew vague details about. Some militants had held Saleem and his colleague's hostage, extorting money and leaving them with permanent scars from relentless beatings– scars that marked his body so deeply, it seemed as though his youth had been forcibly taken away. Saleem, once robust and energetic, now carried the weight of those invisible wounds, his body betraying the vigor it once held.

Saleem, Boba, and I embarked on this journey together. Upon reaching the venue, we were greeted in a manner unique to the culture– elderly women with toothless grins, young women brimming with youthful charm, and some hopeful unmarried girls eyeing their prospects– all came together in chorus, singing the traditional *Wanawun,* a folk melody dedicated to Boba's virtues.

We entered a hall adorned with artificial flowers; their lack of fragrance compensated by the omnipresent aroma of incense sticks. The room was a hive of activity, a crowd of women seated in circular formation. My eyes were drawn to the center where a young man dressed as a woman was dancing to the rhythm of dholak. This was *Laanch,* a man whose seductive moves and coquettish expressions rivalled those of the most playful of maidens. His every twirl and sway were a spectacle, a blend of art and mischief that left everyone mesmerized.

After sometime spent watching the festivities, the bride was taken to her room to be adorned. Each strand of her hair was lovingly tended by different women– amidst this, my attention was caught by something even more fascinating– a subplot unfolding before my eyes.

This was Aakash, the bride's brother, who seemed to bear the entire weight of the wedding on his shoulders. Yet, his purpose extended beyond mere responsibilities. His focus was fixed on a girl with golden hair– Pooja. Every act of service, every errand, was a chance for Aakash to be near her.

The next day, the groom's procession arrived. The groom himself made his entrance on a white horse– one that visibly struggled under his weight, its back arched in surrender. The sight was almost comedic. The man was a heavy-set figure, with long, thick mustaches and frame so broad it seemed God had taken the height meant for him and generously redistributed it into grith instead.

As the bride's family bid farewell, Nitya– the bride– was crying uncontrollably, her sobs shaking her entire being. Her tears were not unwarranted, for she faced the daunting task of carrying the burden of this corpulent man for a lifetime.

This scene took me back to another wedding years ago, in a village when Rubia was married. I remember Ammi had forced me into a three-year old frock and pajama that were far too tight. The pajama tore on the way, and the humiliation ruined the wedding for me. I sat awkwardly with my legs clamped together, unable to enjoy even a single piece of *shirini*– the sweet treats thrown toward the bride. That day when Rubia cried, I had asked Ammi why she wasn't happy?

"It's not easy to leave your home," Ammi had replied. But deep inside I wondered– perhaps, for some, it is easier. Perhaps leaving behind burdens is liberating for others.

The wedding's most memorable moment: was Aadil. On *Maaizraat,* Henna night, it was full of the usual chaos– women laughing, children running around, and the men standing outside, discussing politics and puffing on cigarettes. Saleem was among them, of course, entirely engrossed in his own world. Meanwhile, I was seated among the women, observing everything quietly, when Aadil walked in.

I had heard his name before. Who hadn't? Aadil– the poet whose verses spoke of heartbreak and longing so intense that they felt like they were written just for you. According to Shobha Boba, he was once madly in love with a girl named Rukhsar.

Rukhsar. A name that carried its own scandal. She was mischievous, daring and beautiful in a way that turned heads wherever she went. Aadil had fallen for her completely, a man bounded by the kind of love that consumes you. But their love story didn't end with a happy ever after. Rukhsar betrayed him, or at least that's what everyone said. She ran away with a truck-driver leaving Aadil behind with nothing but his broken heart and unanswered questions. The village gossiped relentlessly about him. "Maybe he wasn't man enough," they whispered, their cruel words attempting to strip him of his dignity. But despite– or perhaps because of– this betrayal, Aadil turned into something of a legend. His heartbreak became the foundation of his art, and his poetry resonated with anyone who had ever known pain.

And there he was, standing in the *aangan,* surrounded by women and young girls who hung on to his every word. He began reciting his poetry, his voice steady yet soulful, each word like a thread pulling deeper into his world.

Then something unexpected happened. Aadil's eyes met mine. It was as if he was searching for something in the crowd, and when he found me, he stopped. His gaze was piercing, unrelenting, and for a moment, I felt like I couldn't breathe.

He paused mid-verse and asked, "Who is she?" his finger pointing directly at me.

Boba, always ready to take charge, placed her hand on my shoulder and said, "This is Noor, Saleem's wife."

Aadil smiled faintly, a smile that didn't quite reach his eyes, and then, in the same rich, hypnotic voice, he said:

"Two skies in Noor's eyes, one dusk, one dawn,

One glows like evening, the other like morn.

Your gaze is a poem, written in fire,

Each glance is verse that takes me higher.

The earth's deep brown, the sea's calm blue,

In your eyes, Noor, a world that's true.

A temple of dreams, a poet's delight,

Your eyes hold the stars, and the moon's soft light."

The women gasped, some giggled, and I... I didn't know what to do. My cheeks burned, and I looked down, hoping to escape the intensity of this gaze.

For the rest of the evening, I avoided Aadil's eyes, but his words stayed with me, they weren't just compliments; they were something more– something that lingered in the air long after he had spoken. In that moment surrounded by the laughter and music of wedding, Aadil made me feel seen in a way I hadn't feel in years. His poetry wasn't just words; it was a mirror, reflecting parts of me I didn't even know existed.

Sixteen

Jeevapur was a quiet place, yet its silence held whispers– of longing, of betrayal, and of the dreams left unsaid. As Saleem's wife, I had learned to adapt to its rhythm. Saleem was a good man hardened by life's trails, but his wounds were not just on his body– they had crept into his soul, making him distant. Our life together was steady and predictable.

Although Saleem had kept things open for me. Whatever I needed, I would tell Boba, and Saleem would give her the money. It was surprising that today, it had been three years and seven months since our marriage. We were close, but it was within a closed room. Every interaction that happened between a husband and wife, we did that but it felt more like a duty. Outside in the world, there was a space, a gap, that make me feel empty. I began to feel the weight of void I couldn't name. Maybe that was the reason why I started paying attention to Aadil.

Few days after the wedding, Boba and I went to the market, as we did every day, to buy vegetables and other stuff, and of course utensils for my newly built kitchen. Boba had given her small patch of her vegetable-growing land to Saleem, where my small palace of three rooms now stood– a place I called *"Hareem-e-Aman"* 'means sanctuary of peace'. I read this name in a magazine that narrated the story of famous warrior from Iran, in which his house was mentioned."

From *Siyah Bakht* to Dayi's house to here, this journey was never easy. Ammi always said, "This world is temporary, just like our place in it." But today, I finally had a beautiful home of my own. Yet, having one thing doesn't mean the whole universe is yours. If everything were attainable, why would people turn to worship? Alongside this achievement, there were gaps– painful absences of those who taught me to dream, to walk, to speak. It was for this kitchen we were shopping for utensils.

While selecting utensils, my gaze wandered across the street. Amid the bustling crowd, a man with curly hair caught my attention. I recognized him immediately– it was Aadil. To my astonishment, he entered the shop we were in. He began conversing in his peculiar poetic manner, speaking to Boba and the shopkeeper, yet carried a layer of meaning, and undercurrent that tugged at something within me. Though his words were directed at others, his glances often strayed in my direction. They weren't invasive, but they stirred something, leaving me unsettled. I tried convincing myself it was nothing more than harmless curiosity. Afterall what could a poet possibly see in me– a woman bound by traditions; her life confined to mundane routines?

That evening, as in stepped out into the *aangan,* I saw him again. He was sitting in the narrow alley with a notebook in hand, scribbling something intently. I hesitated for a moment, but he looked up and smiled– a soft, knowing smile that made my heart skip a beat.

Just then, Boba stepped out of her house. Noticing Aadil, she called out teasingly,

"Aadil, wandering these alleys won't bring you your lost beloved. Come inside." Laughing, she invited him over.

In the *aangan* stood a long wooden bench. Aadil sat down, and Boba began chatting with him. Yet, I could feel his eyes seeking me out, his glances quick but piercing. My heart raced uncontrollably, its rhythm betraying the calm I was struggling to maintain.

In the meantime, Boba went to stoke the fire in her tandoor and said to me, "Noor, you sit here; I'll be back," holding twigs and dried branches in her hand.

"Do you write all day?" I asked, breaking the silence. He looked up, his expression thoughtful. "Not all day. But some words refuse to wait."

I didn't know how to respond, so I turned to leave. But his voice stopped me.

"Noor," He said softly, "Do you know what makes your eyes so extraordinary?"

I froze but didn't turn around. "They are just eyes," I said, attempting to laugh off his words.

"They're not," He insisted. "They're a paradox– one holds the dusk, the other the dawn. They're the kind of eyes poets dream about."

His words stirred something within me– a confusing mix of flattery and unease. I didn't dare look at him. Instead, I walked back inside, heat rushing to my cheeks.

Days turned into weeks, yet I couldn't shake off that moment. Aadil's words lingered– not just because of what he said, but because of how they made me feel. For the first time, I felt seen, as though someone had looked beyond the woman I appeared to be and glimpsed the person I longed to become.

One afternoon, while Saleem was at the market, Aadil appeared at the gate. “I bought these for Saleem,” he said, holding up a bag of fresh pears and camel meat. But I knew it was just an excuse.

“Saleem isn’t home,” I replied curtly.

“Then I’ll leave it with you,” he said, stepping closer.

As he handed me the bag, our fingers brushed for the briefest moment. I quickly pulled my hand away.

“You shouldn’t come here when Saleem isn’t home,” I said firmly.

“I came because I had to,” he replied, his voice low.

“Noor, I can’t stop thinking about you.”

His words stuck me like lightening. A rush of emotions– fear, anger, and something I couldn’t name– overwhelmed me.

“You’re crossing a line,” I whispered, my voice trembling.

“I know,” he admitted, but sometimes the heart doesn’t care about lines. Noor, you are the most beautiful thing I’ve ever known– not just your eyes, but your silence, your strength. You deserve to hear that.”

I didn’t respond, but my silence seemed to embolden him. “Let me say this, and I’ll never bother you again,” he pleaded.

“Your eyes– they’re a story. Every time I look at them, I feel like I’m reading a poem I’ll never fully understand.”

Unable to face him, I turned away. “Leave, Aadil,” I said, my voice shaking. “This isn’t right.”

Boba, who was kneeling by the tandoor making *lawasa,* noticed the exchange. I joined her to escape the moment. Smiling slyly, she teased. So, did you like the poet’s verses, or poet himself?”

I laughed nervously, brushing it off. “Boba, I’m married,” I said, hoping to end the conversation.

Blowing smoke from her hookah, she replied,

“Love changes empires, child. You’re just a person. Don’t take offense, but let me tell you something. Saleem is a good man. At your age, the risk of slipping is high. My wisdom didn’t come with age and scars. Distant flowers always seem more beautiful. Sometimes, cruelty and kindness are just two sides of the same tree. Saleem may be harsh, but he will stand by you. Don’t let fleeting weeds ruin your crops.”

Her words stung. I felt my face flush with anger, though I couldn’t quite understand why. I didn’t know if it was her wisdom on her insinuation that cause the fury inside me. I wanted to argue, but instead, I silently avoided her gaze, focusing on the *lawasa* she was preparing.

That night, as I sat in the dimly lit room watching Saleem sleep, the weight of my life settled over me. His face bore the marks of struggles I couldn't fathom, his breathing heavy with the exhaustion of battles I would never fully understand. I wanted to love him, but in that moment, I felt the ache of love I could never give– a love that didn't belong to the life we shared.

And yet, Aadil's words echoed in my mind like a forbidden melody. I knew I had to bury them, let them die in the silence of my heart. But as I closed my eyes, his words came alive once more:

"Your eyes are storm waiting to break,

A poem unraveled in twilight's wake.

One carries the dusk, the other the dawn,

A dance of light where shadows are drawn."

In that fleeting moment, I felt alive and lost, caught between the love I owed and the love I could never claim.

The days shifted on in a haze. I couldn't put my finger on why I felt so restless. The chill was in the air, the mountains still covered in snow, but the streets, the ground were engulfed in a thick fog. I kept finding myself staring down the narrow alley, as if waiting for someone, though I couldn't quite say who. I had been waiting for something, but what? My thoughts were a tangled mess.

Then, on the thirteenth day, I saw Aadil again, surrounded by women, his voice rising with pride as he recited his poetry. It was a scene I had witnessed many times before, but today, there was something different about it. I couldn't explain it, but it gnawed at me.

Saleem and I were headed to the market to buy some goods. As we passed by, I caught a glimpse of Aadil. Our eyes met for a fleeting second– just enough to send a jolt through me. I felt like something was shifting in the air, something I couldn't understand. We picked up our things, but when we returned, he was gone.

That same day, I saw him again sitting with a girl on the same corner of the street. I felt a tightness in my chest, an unfamiliar ache. Without thinking I opened the door to my house and went inside. Something inside me had shifted, but I wasn't sure if it was for better or worse.

Days passed. Saleem was busy with work, and I was left alone, caught in whirlwind of emotions. He was going away for business, leaving Boba in charge of me, just he always did. Aadil, however, continued to appear, though I tried to ignore him. But when Saleem was away, I couldn't resist. I made up an excuse to visit Ilma, one of my neighbors, and once again found myself meeting Aadil on the same corner. His poetic words felt like a trap, a lur I couldn't resist. His voice was like honey, each word wrapping around me, pulling me closer into his web.

One evening, Aadil and I visited the shrine of Habba Khatoon, a poetess whose verses Ammi used to hum to lull me to sleep. I always wondered, if her words were so enchanting, what kind of personality she must have had. Aadil told me her story. She had loved deeply and tragically, and it seemed as if her spirit lingered in the very air around us.

The tension between Aadil and me built slowly, like a storm gathering in the distance. And then, one day, the storm broke.

I had heard of Laleshwari, a poetess with a tragic love story, and Aadil had told me about her too. But it wasn't her story that haunted me now; it was my own. The day, I had an argument with Aadil, a moment of unspoken anger that had boiled over. As I stormed out of the house, my mind was a blur, my emotions a whirlpool of confusion.

As I entered the house, Saleem's voice thundered from behind.

"Where have you been all this time? Where did you go today?"

I froze, not knowing how to respond. His anger was a heavy eight passing down on me. But then, something snapped inside me. I turned to face him and answered.

"I was at Ilma's house, Sabar!"

Saleem didn't say another word. He simply walked away, heading out to the market, his coat pulled tight against the cold. I stood there, feeling a strange mix of fear and defiance.

Boba was sitting by the tandoor, working as usual. She had always been a quiet presence in my life, but today something was different. She didn't ask me anything. Instead, she quietly sat next to me, her voice calm but filled with an unspoken understanding.

"Noor, Ilma came by today with her husband. She said her husband saw you and Aadil together at shrine."

My heart raced, the truth settling in like a stone in my chest.

Boba continued, her voice soft but heavy with meaning. "Saleem is like a son to me. He's had a hard life, you know? His mother died when he was seven, and at eleven, he buried his father. His family betrayed him, and that pain...it never goes away."

I could feel the weight of Boba's words, but they didn't change what had happened. I was still caught in the web of my own choices, and I knew deep down that I had crossed a line I could never return from.

Later that night, Saleem came home. He was silent his anger still simmering beneath the surface. He didn't say a word as he lay down and drifted off to sleep. But I couldn't sleep. The weight of what I had done pressed on me like a thousand-kilo stone.

The night was cold, and in the stillness, memories Ammi flooded back to me. I remembered her words, her wisdom. And now in the darkness, I understood her better than I ever had before.

The next morning, I woke to the sound of the rooster crowing. I watched my face, prayed *Salah,* and then joined Boba at tandoor. As we worked together, I felt an overwhelming need to confess everything.

"Boba," I whispered, my voice thick with guilt. "I am guilty.

It was a trap, and I didn't know how to get out. What will Saleem Sahab do now? Will he leave me?"

Tears welled up in my eyes as I spoke.

"I slapped Aadil that day," I continued. "He touched me, and I thought it was an accident. But then, he kept pushing. He tried to hug me, and I pushed him away. He fell, and then he started shouting... Calling me names. 'You came to me, you slut. Didn't Saleem satisfy you? What were you doing here with me, cooking up a whorehouse for me? 'His words hit me like a slap, and I couldn't stop the tears. I had lost everything. My respect, my dignity... all gone."

Boba gaze softened, but there was no pity in her eyes. She simply nodded. "Noor, women like us are subjects in stories. Some are true, some are lies. Aadil is nothing but a moth, drawn to the flame. Saleem is like Rohit to me he has his flaws, but he's a good man. You're lucky to have him."

I listened, the words sinking deep into my soul.

"*Wafa* is a small word," Boba continued. "But living it? That's the real challenge. You'll see. And remember this: a woman's life is built on two names– her own, and the name of her husband."

As Boba spoke, I realized how much I had to learn. I had thought I understood love, but now, I saw how naïve I had been. The *bunyaad* Ammi spoke of was loyalty, faithfulness. I had betrayed that trust, and now I had to face the consequences.

In my heart, I knew it was too late to turn back. I had lost everything, and today, I could no longer look at myself the same way. But perhaps, somewhere deep within me, I could rebuild. Maybe. The room was quiet except for the soft crackle of the fire. I sat near the *chula* in the kitchen, staring into its glow, unsure of what to say. Saleem was beside me, his gaze fixed on the flames, his face calm but unreadable. The weight of everything hung heavy in the air, but he didn't speak of it, didn't mention the cracks I had caused. Instead, he handed me a small cup of salt tea without a word, his fingers brushing mine briefly. It was an ordinary gesture, yet it held something unspoken—something I wasn't sure I deserved.

"Drink," he said simply, his voice steady.

I took the cup, feeling the warmth seep into my hands, and sipped in silence. For the first time in what felt like forever, the tea didn't taste bitter.

Saleem broke the silence, his tone light, almost as if we had been talking about nothing at all. "Azmat– his coworker, is coming tomorrow," he said. "He's bringing the seeds."

I looked at him, surprised by the sudden change in topic. "Seeds?"

"For the mustard," he replied, leaning back against the wall. "It's almost time to sow them. If we start now, we'll have *haakh*– a dish made from the leaves of mustard plant, ready before the first snowfall."

The thought of mustard leaves, tender and green, cooked into a thick, delicious curry with fresh corn flatbread on the side, made my heart ache with nostalgia. Ammi used to make it every winter, her hands working deftly over the *chula* as she hummed softly to herself.

Saleem glanced at me, a faint smile playing on his lips. "You'll help, won't you?"

I nodded; my throat tight. "Ji," I whispered.

The door creaked open just then, and Boba stepped inside, her sturdy frame filling the small space. She carried a bundle of firewood over one shoulder and set it down by the wall with a grunt. "The night's getting colder," she said, rubbing her hands together. "But the moon's bright enough to light the whole valley." She turned to us, her sharp eyes taking in the scene—the fire, the tea, the unspoken tension hanging between us. But Boba, in her wisdom, said nothing of it. Instead, she lowered herself onto the small wooden bench with a satisfied sigh.

"What's this I hear about mustard?" she asked, her voice warm and familiar.

Saleem chuckled softly. "We were just talking about it. Noor's going to help this time."

Boba raised an eyebrow at me, a playful glint in her eye. "You? In the fields? I'll believe it when I see it."

I managed a small smile, the lightness of her tone easing something inside me. "I'll prove you wrong, Boba. Just wait."

She nodded approvingly, her weathered face softening. "Good. We'll need strong hands this season. The fields aren't kind to the weak."

For a moment, the three of us sat in companionable silence, the warmth of the fire wrapping around us like a shared blanket. Then Boba spoke again, her tone thoughtful.

"You know, mustard's a tricky thing," she said, looking at the fire as if it held all the wisdom of the world. "You have to sow it carefully, space the seeds just right. Too close, and they choke each other. Too far, and they don't grow strong enough to withstand the cold."

She paused, her gaze flickering to me. "But if you do it right, Noor, you get something beautiful. Something that feeds not just the body, but the soul."

I nodded, her words settling over me like a gentle balm. "I'll do my best, Boba."

She smiled, his eyes crinkling at the corners. "That's all anyone can ask."

The conversation drifted to other things—plans for the fields, stories of past harvests, the simple joys of life in the valley. And as I listened to their voices, something inside me began to heal.

Perhaps the past couldn't be undone. Perhaps the wounds I had caused would take time to mend. But in that moment, surrounded by warmth and laughter, I felt a flicker of hope.

Maybe, just maybe, we could sow something new.

Seventeen

Masha Allah, Saleem and Boba are the reason all my embroidery suits sold today. Saleem's striking red cheeks and strong Pashtun like build always drew people to my little stall in the market. He'd stand tall beside me, calling out to passerby,

"See these delicate stiches? She has made them herself!" his pride in my work was something that kept me going, even when life felt heavy. Boba, meanwhile, would sit at her tandoor all week, her hands hardened from years of kneading dough, her spirit still strong despite the weight of her age.

One Friday, I gave Saleem a white prayer cap with hand-embroidered borders I had stitched myself. When Saleem returned from prayers, he asked, "Where did you buy this?"

I replied, "I made it." He was surprised and said, "Everyone praised it. Why didn't you ever tell me you could do this?"

I replied, "Ammi taught me. Whenever I had time here, I would do embroidery, and I embroidered your cap to match your kurta."

Saleem, excited, said, "This should be in the market!" and that's how my business of hand-embroidered suits began.

Every Saturday and Sunday, I sold my suits in the bustling *bazaar.* It was there, on one such day, that I first met Aagha Dilawer. A tall, thin, bald man dressed in pants and shirt, with short grey beard, wearing glasses, holding a pen and diary in one hand, and a cigar tucked behind his ear. He approached slowly, drawn, it seemed, by the intricate embroidery on one of my kurtas, the one on which I engraved with colorful threads the words–

"Alif Laam Meem," the very first word of the first chapter of the Quraan.

"These are beautiful," he said, his voice smooth but curious. "Your hands must be magical."

I smiled politely. "It's just practice," I replied, arranging the suits neatly.

His gaze lingered, and then he said, almost to himself, "Your eyes... they are mesmerizing. Where are you from? Are you from Iran?"

"Kashmir," I said softly, looking down at the fabric in my hands.

"Where in Kashmir?"

"Kahsar Pur," I answered without thinking.

His expressions changed; the casual curiosity replaced by something sharper. “Kahsar Pur?” he repeated.

“Isn’t this the same mysterious village where a young couple was brutally set on fire by assailants? I covered that news when they were brought to a hospital here.”

I stiffened. “I don’t talk about that place anymore.”

“But you should,” he said leaning in slightly.

“People need to hear the truth.”

I didn’t respond. Instead, I packed up my suits and walked away, my hands trembling.

When I returned home that evening, Saleem was already there. Waiting on the bench in *aangan*. He was chopping vegetables for dinner, his strong hands moving with practiced ease.

“You’re late,” he said without looking up.

“The market was busy,” I replied, sitting down slowly, my swollen belly making every moment deliberate. He put his knife down and looked at me.

“You look tired.”

"I'm fine," I said, though I wasn't. the weight of Aagha's questions and the memories stirred was suffocating.

Saleem moved closer, kneeling in front of me. His hands rested gently on my belly.

"Is the baby kicking today?"

I nodded, and as if on cue, a soft kick startled me. I laughed despite myself. "This one is impatient as you."

Saleem smiled, but his eyes were clouded with worry.

"Noor, you have to take care of yourself, as Dr. Saloni Sahiba said. There should be no thoughts in your mind that could affect the body. God forbid; I won't be able to bear another tragedy."

"I met someone today," I said hesitantly. "A journalist. He asked about Kahsar Pur."

"Noor," Saleem said firmly, "you know what happens when you dig into the past. The past is like a spider's web; the more you delve into it, the more you lose the present. Those who live in the present are the ones who are truly happy. Don't let anyone drag you into it."

The next few days passed uneventfully. I spent most of my time with Boba, helping her at the tandoor while Saleem worked in the *Sabzi Mandi.* But on Wednesday, everything changed.

Saleem didn't came home. I waited until nightfall, pacing the small room, my heart pounding. When I finally stepped outside to ask the neighbors, I was met with silence and unease glances.

"They took him," someone whispered.

"Who?" I demanded, my voice rising.

"The agency," they said before hurrying away.

My knees buckled; I clutched the wall for support. Saleem Lala– my Saleem– had been taken. And for what? Because he looked like an Afghani? Because he was a proud, strong man who never bent to anyone's will?

Boba took me to the house, and she slept there. I was lost in thought, worried and troubled.

Boba said, "trust in God, he is safe. He will come back in morning. Now, go to sleep."

Strange thoughts kept crossing my mind. God forbid, what if something happened to Saleem? After such a long time, we had built such a *bunyaad*– why, God, why?

I placed my hand on my belly and got lost in my thought. As the night grew deeper, I remembered that time when I had strayed, caught up in Aadil's false and manipulative words. And then Saleem, how he forgave my huge mistake as if nothing had ever happened. Maybe that's why we became so close to each other. After that we started living a better and happier life together. God, why did such a calamity fall upon me again?

Those days without Saleem were the darkest of my life. I couldn't eat, couldn't sleep. The baby's kicks became more frequent, as if it too was restless, sensing my despair. I spend my nights staring at the ceiling, my mind racing with fears of what they might be doing to him.

Boba moved into my house during that time, refusing to leave me alone.

"You're not going through this by yourself," she said firmly.

On the fourth night, we decided to make *harissa* for dinner, something to keep our hand busy and our minds distracted. As the rich aroma filled the house, I felt a momentary sense of calm. Boba hummed softly, her voice a balm to my frayed nerves. But the calm shattered with the sound of screams from the street. The riots erupted without warning. A political rally had turned violent, and now the flames of hatred were consuming Jeevapur. Houses were being set on fire, the inhabitants dragged out and beaten.

Boba and I hurdled in the kitchen, the pot of *harissa* forgotten. "Stay inside," I whispered, my voice shaking. The shouts grew louder, closer. Someone banged on the door, and my heart stopped.

"Noor," Boba said, her voice trembling "Stay inside, don't go out."

She grabbed my hand and led me to the small storage room at the back of my house. "Stay here. Don't come out until say it's safe."

I told Boba to stay behind, pulling her arm back, "I will handle it," though h I had no idea how.

I stepped back into the main room just as the door burst open. A group of men stormed in; their faces twisted with rage.

"Where's the man of the house?" one of them demanded.

"He is not here," I said, standing my ground despite the terror coursing through me.

One of the men sneered. "No husband, and yet you're pregnant? What kind of woman are you?"

I felt my blood boil. "The kind of woman who will protect her home, just like your sister and mother, no matter what."

They laughed, but before they could say anything more, a loud whistle echoed from outside. "The Army's coming!" someone shouted.

The men fled, their bravado trembling. I locked the door behind them, my hands shacking.

Boba emerged from the storage room, her face pale.

"Noor, you're brave, but don't ever do that again."

I didn't respond. I simply collapsed into a chair, my hands resting on my belly. For the first time in days, I felt the baby kick gently, as if reassuring me that we would survive this– together.

Nine days has passed, and I was sitting in the *aangan,* counting the hours, the minutes, the seconds since Saleem had been taken. The sun hung heavy in the sky; its warmth unable to pierce the cold fear that had settled in my chest.

And I saw him.

Saleem was walking slowly down the alley, his steps uneven, his shoulders slumped. His clothes were torn, his face hollow. It was as if the world had drained him of all his strength. My heart stopped for a moment, and then my eyes filled with tears– tears that spilled over uncontrollably as I struggled to breathe. I wanted to run to him, to hold him, but I couldn't move. My body, heavy with pregnancy and days of despair, refused to obey. Instead, I sat there on the bench, sobbing, my hands clutching my belly as if to shield our child from the pain.

"Saleem," I whispered, my voice cracking under the weight of my emotions.

He reached the gate and stopped. Looking at me with eyes that seemed older, wearier. "Noor," he said, his voice barely audible.

I finally managed to stand, stumbling toward him. When I reached him, I placed my hands on his chest, as if to confirm he was real. The moment I felt his heartbeat, I broke down, my forehead pressing against him as my tears soaked his shirt.

"They hurt you," I said between sobs. "They hurt you because of how you look, because they think they can."

He placed his hand on my head, his touch trembling but gentle. "Noor, I'm here how. That's all that matters. I'm here with you."

Deep down, I knew the storm wasn't over. Jeevapur had become a battlefield, and our survival would depend on the strength of our love and the truths we choose to fight for.

Boba emerged from her house across the *aangan*, her frail frame rushing towards us faster than I thought possible. "Saleem!" she cried, her voice thick with relief.

He turned to her, offering a small, tired smile. "Poph."

She grabbed his arm, pulling him toward the bench where I had been sitting. "Sit down, my son. You look like you've been through hell."

He winced as he lowered himself onto the bench. "They kept me asking questions, they wanted to know who I was, where I was from. They kept saying I look like an Afghani, as if that was a crime."

Boba clicked her tongue, her eyes blazing with anger.

"Those shaitaan! They don't need a reason to hurt people. They just do it because they can. But look at you– you're alive. Shivji has bought you back to us." Boba believed in Lord Shiva. When Saleem was taken away, she used to pray for him in her prayer room, which was always filled with the fragrance of incense sticks, and a small oil lamp remained lit all the times. Boba believed that lamp's extinction meant the world's end, so I sometimes added oil to it for her.

I knelt in front of him, my hands wrapping around his. "Saleem, you have to promise me. Promise me you'll be careful. I can't lose you again."

He looked into my eyes, his own filled with unshed tears. "I promise. But we can't live in fear. Not for ourselves, and not for our child."

His hands moved to my belly, where our baby gave a soft kick, as if sensing its father's touch. A small smile broke through my tears.

Boba placed her hand on both of ours. "This family will stay together," she said firmly. "No matter what happens, we will face it together."

In the days that followed, we tried to return to normalcy, but Jeevapur was still reeling from the riots. Boba's tandoor and the mesh cage of ducks had been smashed by rioters– a deliberate act of hatred.

One morning Saleem and I stood in the *aangan,* looking at the ruins of the tandoor and missing the quacking sounds of the ducks. Boba came out, her eyes scanning the destruction with a mix of sadness and determination.

"We'll rebuilt it," Saleem said firmly.

"How?" boba asked. "The bricks are broken; the tools are gone, ducks are gone; everything is gone."

"No," I said, stepping closer to her. "Not everything. We're still here, Boba. As long as we are here, we can start again."

That weekend, we began the work. Saleem gathered bricks from the debris while I mixed the mud, sitting carefully to avoid straining myself. Boba supervised, her sharp eyes catching every detail. Neighbors came to help, bringing tools and supplies, some brought a few ducklings for a new cage. Their solidarity a balm against the wounds of the riots.

As we worked, I felt something shift within me– not just the baby, who kicked more frequently now, but a sense of hope. Jeevapur had tried to break us, but we were still standing, still fighting, still holding on to each other.

The tandoor and the cage were rebuilt, Boba's smile returned as the aroma of *lawasa* and her hookah filled the *aangan.*

That evening we sat in the *aangan.* I leaned on Saleem's shoulder, the fire crackling softly. Boba took occasional sips from her hookah, the soft *gud gud*... sound filling the air, as she shared stories from her past with us. We had lost something, but we still had each other. We never made it to the headlines of newspapers. And that was enough to begin again.

Eighteen

In Kahsar Pur, whispers spread like wildfire. The endless said sins had consumed the land, and that was why the rains had forsaken them. Drought had parched the fields, and despair had taken root in every heart. A few days ago, the sun had been swallowed by a mysterious angel, a myth I only came to understand here in Jeevapur, when I read about it in a fifth-grade geography book of Ilma's daughter Sara– it was called an eclipse.

Villagers claimed that it was a punishment– a celestial wrath for the transgression of man. I had overheard Dayi and Ammi whispering about it, their voices heavy with fear and reverence, blaming the sins of people for this divine retribution.

The day of the *grahan,* eclipse, was unlike any I had seen before. We were in the fields when the world suddenly dimmed. The light faded, and the eerie shadow began to stretch across the sky. The air thickened with an unnatural silence, and my vision swirled as though the earth itself was tilting. Ammi rushed to me, her face pale, her dupatta hurriedly pulled over my head. Without a word, she scooped me into her arms and began running toward home. I could feel her heart racing as she held me tightly.

When we reached the safety of our home, I mustered the courage to ask, "Ammi, why is this happening?"

Her eyes widened, and she shushed me sharply. "Noor, don't you dare look at the sun today! It is cursed– an angel has captured it because of the sins of humanity." Her voice dropped to a whisper.

"Stay inside Noor. Even the shadow of this day can harm you."

I was looking at Ammi, her worried eyes fixed on me, her *shahada* finger repeatedly pointing in my direction, as if urging me to understand something. I was caught in a web of confusion, wondering whether *suhaga* (borax) which was occasionally spread on our door would cause more harm than this or less.

Just then, Ammi added, her voice tinged with both fear and belief, "Have you seen Zahida? Her cleft lip and that long black moon like mark on her belly? That's because her mother didn't protect her from the last *grahan."*

I was too young to understand the weight of her words, but the fear in her voice etched that day into my memory.

Along with the mystery of solar eclipse, Ammi had also shared once with me an intriguing secret about the moon. Once, Ammi had pointed out a ring around the moon, explaining its secrets to me. "If the ring is close to the moon, rains will come. But if it's far, the land will remain dry," she had said. That night, as we walked from Dayi's house, the dark sky held no such promise of rain.

The drought opened, and with it, the villagers' desperation. The men and women, young and old, began gathering for prayers, pleading for heavens to open. They believed fervently in the power of collective repentance. For me, though, it wasn't the prayer that excited me– it was the *halwa.* Eleven times they made it, and eleven time the sweet, nutty aroma filled the air, teasing my senses. I secretly wished that drought wasn't just a harbinger of sweets. Fire became a frequent visitor in the village. The fields, already brittle from dryness, were set ablaze– some by the hashish smokers and some by sun's merciless heat. Ammi called them sinners, those who burned fields initially, robbing birds, insects, and small creatures of their homes and lives. To her, the greatest sin was to steal the right to live from God's creatures.

I saw Ammi in tears as she spoke about *Gowbe, (*Dung beetle) how it tirelessly rolls and collects dung to build its home. She expressed how, despites its hard work, we humans destroy its homes just like we destroy the nests of birds, causing them to burn.

One day, flames licked the edge of our field. I stood in the *aangan,* watching helplessly as smoke spiraled into the sky. Villagers rushed to extinguish the fire but failed. Then I saw Ammi, her silhouette framed against the fiery backdrop. In her hands, she held branches from the *Kachnar* tree– the same tree she had named Noori and marked six circular lines to measure my growing height. Ammi plunged into the blaze with a ferocity I'd never seen before. She fought the fire around the tree as if she were protecting her own child. Her dupatta was singed, her hands blackened with soot, but she didn't stop until the flames were gone. The fields were reduced to ash, but the tree stood unscathed, its leaves trembling as though in gratitude.

From the *aangan,* I heard Parveen's mocking voice. "Mad woman," she sneered. But Ammi paid no heed. That night as we sat together– Dayi, Ammi and I– I couldn't contain my curiosity. "Ammi why did you protect that tree? Just one tree?"

Ammi remained silent; her eyes distant. It was Dayi who answered, her voice soft yet firm. "Noor, your Ammi is a woman of deep love and conviction. I understand in her ways you can't yet. One day you will grow up and understand too."

I looked at Ammi, searching her face for answers. Her silence spoke of strength I couldn't yet grasp, a connection to the world that transcended logic. That night I dreamt of the tree, its roots wrapped around my heart, whispering secrets I wasn't ready to hear.

Today, outside the *aangan,* the halwa ceremony was in full swing. The voice of neighborhood mingled with the faint clinking of plates and the laughter of children. Every new guest was greeted warmly, with Saleem Lala's booming voice ringing out, "Khair Mubarak!" It was a day of joy and celebration that stretched beyond the walls of our home and into the heart of those who had gathered.

For me, this day was monumental– a day etched in my soul. I had given birth to a son. My son a miracle wrapped in soft delicate skin. I lay on the bed, my body still heavy with exhaustion, yet my heart light with an emotion I couldn't quite name. Saleem would be happy, wouldn't he? Though I knew deep down, he had wanted a girl.

The baby's cooing brought me back from my thoughts. Gently I turned to my side, the slight ache in my body still a reminder of a storm I had weathered last night. I extended my *shahada* finger towards him, and with a soft, instinctual grip, his tiny hand closed around it. I felt the warmth of his fragile fingers and the lump rose in my throat. His face was so small, so perfect as though sculped by a divine hand.

Last night felt like a lifetime ago. The pain had come in waves, relentless and unyielding, each contraction tearing through me as though my body were being remade from within. Saleem and Boba has rushed me to nearby hospital, their voices urgent yet trembling with hope.

In the dim hospital room, time had blurred. The world outside ceased to exist, and all that mattered was the battle within me. It felt like an eternity, as though I were suspended between life and death. I clung to the words Ammi has always whispered to me in times of despair: “after every hardship, there is ease.” Those words are my anchor, my prayer, my desperate hope.

And then suddenly, the storm passed. The pain receded, leaving in its wave of serenity. I heard it before I saw him– the first cry of my child, piercing the silence of the room like the sweetest melody. The ease had come, just as Ammi had promised.

Now, lying on the bed, I felt a tear slide down my cheek as I watched him, this tiny being who had been a part of me for so long. His every breath felt like a miracle, his every movement a testament to the strength it had taken to bring him into his world.

Outside, the voice of celebration continued, a background symphony to my quiet moment of awe. The aroma of freshly roasted halwa wafted through the air, mingling with the scent of new life. For now, I was content to simply lie there, my finger in his grasp, marveling at the ease that had finally arrived.

I was lost in the mix of half dreams when Boba entered the room. She carried a bowl in her hands, and the scent of halwa wafted through the air, filling the space with a warmth that felt almost maternal. It was as if Boba had sensed my longing for it, as though she had read my thoughts. Her face glowed with a joy so deep it seemed to have smoothed away at least a wrinkle or two, softening the line of age carved by years of life. Dressed in neat, clean clothes, she came straight to my bed, her hand steady but her voice trembling with excitement. She played a gentle hand on my forehead, kissed it tenderly, and said, "Mubarak, Noor."

Her smile deepened, her words brimming with pride. "And Mubarak to me too– I have become a grandmother! Nani." She held out the bowl, and rich aroma of halwa enveloped me.

"Here, have some. Saleem made it himself. The boy is over the moon, so much so that he's out distributing sweets to the entire neighborhood!"

Her laughter rang soft and sweet as she added, "Come, let me help you sit up."

Carefully, she helped me into a seated position, her hand firm yet delicate, as though holding something precious. I began eating the halwa, each bite melting on my tongue like the moment itself– sweet, fleeting, and perfect.

Boba moved to other side of the bed, her face softening even further as her eyes fell on the baby. She reached out, plucked an eyelash from her own lid, and placed on the baby's forehead– a timeless gesture of love and protection. Then, with a faint mischievous glimmer in her eye, she lifted the hem of her outer garment to reveal another layer beneath– a faded green layer with a hidden pocket, she reached into it and pulled out a tiny shimmering silver bangle, its surface catching the light. Her hands shook slightly and she held it out, her voice breaking with emotion. "This is for my grandson," she whispered, her pride as evident as the tears threatening to spill from her eyes.

"Noor, just look at him! My God, he's the spitting image of you. Look at his eyes!"

Her words awakened a memory in me. The bangle reminded me of the knitted cap Ammi had made with her own hands.

"Boba, I said softly, there is a cap in the top shelf of the cupboard, in the far corner. Could you put it on him? It's the only thing I have left of Ammi, apart from the memories."

Boba's face grew seriously and she walked over the cupboard, handling the cap with reverence when she found it. She placed it gently on the baby's tiny head, her face breaking into smile so wide it made her look ten years younger. "Noor", she said suddenly, her voice filled with wonder, "you know, I didn't take a single puff from my hookah today. I didn't want even a trace of tobacco's scent to reach my grandson."

I smiled back at her, my heart full of gratitude for her small, beautiful sacrifices. Her happiness felt like a warm, steady glow that filled the room, touching everything and everyone in it.

She stood up, adjusting her clothes, as if to shake of her emotions. "I should start preparing g dinner," she said glancing at the window. "We'll have more guests by evening. If you need anything just call me from the window. I'll in the *aangan."* With that she left, leaving behind an unshakable sense of love. As I savored each bite of halwa, a smile played on my lips. Ammi's words echoed in my mind, "Put yourself in someone else's shoe to understand them better."

Today I finally understood what she truly meant. My journey through childhood had ended, and new chapter was unfolding. It was no longer about me– it was about watching my child's journey, just as Ammi had watched mine, shaping me with love, patience, and wisdom. Now it was my turn to do the same.

Lost in my thoughts, I didn't notice when Saleem walked in. his warm greeting, "Salaam," brought me back. He sat down, not on a chair but at the foot of my bed, looking directly at me with an expression that melted my heart. He placed the bowl of halwa from my hand on the window sill, took my hand gently and said with raw emotion, "thank you, Noor. And thank God."

Hesitatingly, I asked, "are you happy?"

His eyes widened as if in disbelief, and with a radiant smile, he replied, "more than I can ever express."

He reached into the pocket of his black kameez and pulled out a folded piece of paper. "Look," he said, unfolding it, "I went to Qari Sahab for name suggestions. He gave me three. You have to choose one, and in the meantime, let me meet my little prince."

Saleem placed the paper on my lap and turned towards the baby. From his pocket he pulled out a few rupee notes and waved over the baby, a symbolic gesture of warding of the evil eye. Then he bent down, kissed the baby gently, and held him close. Tears welled up in his eyes and began streaming down his cheeks. When the baby started crying softly, he carefully placed him in my lap and said, "Noor you and Boba have no idea how much running I did today. We've been to the market three times getting everything you and the baby need. Once you feel better, we'll sort through it all."

I could see the happiness etched on his face, in his every word and movement. Then he sat closer, his voice thick with emotions. "Noor, you don't know how important this day is for me– for us. By god's grace I'll provide the best life for our child."

I unfolded the paper. It had three names: Basim, Rashid and Saad. Saad was written in heavy, bold ink.

"I like Saad," I said softly. "What does it mean?"

"It means a pillar, a support," he replied.

I nodded. "Then it's perfect but you decide."

He laughed; his joy unmistakable. "I knew it! I knew you'd choose the same name as me. Saad it is!"

Overcome with the excitement, Saleem rushed outside to share the news: "Saad is the name of newborn!"

His usual calmness was replaced with childlike joy as he organized the baby's bedding while Boba helped me feed Saad.

Saleem glanced at Boba and said, "Once Saad is older, we'll visit Kahsar Pur. Noor has so many memories there, and I want Saad to be a part of them."

Boba nodded, and they insisted I rest, talking and planning nearby, their voices soothing background to my tired mind.

As I closed my eyes, exhaustion washing over me, my thoughts drifted to Ammi. Memories of my childhood played like an old movie reel, vivid and comforting. Saad has inherited Ammi's eyes– exactly like hers, as if she were watching me through him.

In that quite moment, I made a promise to myself: I will raise Saad just like Ammi raised me. Patience, gratitude, perseverance, resilience– these would be the pillars of his character, just as they were mine. I realized, with a profound sense of gratitude, that the greatest day in parent's life is when their child says, "I want to be like you."

Today, I whispered to myself, Noor, you will be like Ammi. I will teach Saad everything, just as she taught me.

As I drifted into sleep, I knew this was just a beginning. Saad's journey would be my purpose, my pride, and my legacy. Just like

Ammi, I would give without measure, love without condition, and stand as his pillar– his Saad.

THE PATH FORWARD

As Noor's journey comes to an end, it leaves behind a trail of questions, courage, and quiet revolutions in the hearts of those who have walked beside her. Feminism is not just a banner for change; it is a whisper in every woman's soul that she is enough, that she has the right to dream, to resist, to shine. Noor's story is a reminder that women are not defined by the weight of expectations placed upon them, but by the fire they carry within—the courage to question, the resilience to endure, and the strength to rise. Women's empowerment isn't about granting power; it is about acknowledging the power that has always existed, buried beneath centuries of silence and submission. Noor's journey is every woman's journey—a testament to the quiet, unyielding strength that reshapes societies and redefines freedom. To the readers, I leave this: let Noor's voice echo in your heart, and may her resilience inspire you to see, hear, and celebrate the Noor in every woman. The world doesn't change when one woman rises; it changes when we all rise together.

A Note to My Readers

Thank you for journeying this far. Your presence here is a testament to the connection we've shared through these words, and I'm profoundly grateful for it.

This world I've woven is not bound by reality; it exists in the realm of imagination- an endless expanse where depth is defined by how far your mind dares to wander. Every word penned was an invitation to explore, to feel and to envision something beyond the tangible.

What you've read is not merely a story but a reflection of how vividly one can dream. If, at any moment, my words resonated with your thoughts or stirred an emotion within you, then this endeavor has fulfilled its purpose.

As you reach the end, remember; this world now belongs to you. It will be as profound, limitless, and meaningful as your imagination allows it to be.

Thank you once again, for walking this path with me. Without you, these words would remain incomplete- a melody unheard, a vision unseen.

I would be delighted to hear your feedback. Feel free to share your thoughts with me at xavithefalcon@gmail.com

Scan the QR code above to connect with me on LinkedIn.

With gratitude,

A seeker of words, a weaver of dreams.

www.ingramcontent.com/pod-product-compliance
Lightning Source LLC
Chambersburg PA
CBHW031521180726
48282CB00056B/195